Mr Roopratna's Chocolate

Mr Roopratna's Chocolate

The winning stories from the
1999 Rhys Davies Competition

seren

seren
is the book imprint of
Poetry Wales Press Ltd
Wyndham Street, Bridgend, Wales

ISBN 1-85411-267-8

A CIP record for this title is available from
the British Library

*The publisher works with the financial assistance of the
Arts Council of Wales*

Published with the assistance of

THE RHYS DAVIES TRUST

Printed in Plantin by CPD Wales, Ebbw Vale

Contents

Catherine Merriman

Painting Juliet

'What is it about plants?' Juliet asked, after the dozenth time I refused to paint her portrait.

I plucked a herbaceous attribute from the air. 'The stillness,' I said.

A good one. She didn't know whether to freeze, vegetable-like, or rant, her-like.

She wants me to paint her portrait. I'm not that kind of artist, I say. Not any more. I'm capable of it, of course, but I never paint girlfriends. Even frisky, amusing, twenty-eight-year-old girlfriends, who take inexplicable shines to middle-aged daubers. Call it tact, if you like. Or cowardice. I draw plants, not portraits. A portrait is a front(ish) view of a human being. Artists, despite our fleeting delusions, are mere humans too, and human beings interact. Juliet and I have been interacting for several months. If I paint her portrait, I won't be painting an object, which just happens to be a person. I'll be painting a relationship.

Not a problem with plants. Interaction is not one of their strengths. Obligingly passive, undemanding things. Perfect sitters. They don't give a toss what they look like, leaves all askew, the odd petal droop – a matter of total indifference. They're happy to hold a pose for hours, or not hold it; they don't get miffed if you decide to take photos and work from them instead. You don't have to talk to them, though you can, of course, if you must, and their discretion is absolute. Nor do they object if you have a fag or a drink without offering them one, or fart or belch in their presence.

And, you know, there's a lot more demand for pictures of plants than of people. Oh yes. Take a look in your book shelves. How many gardening books have you got? Plant identification books? Nature books? Use a lot of sketches, paintings, don't they? Now, how many books of human portraits have you got? None? Thought so. We all have a living to make.

I am sketching a nice docile yucca at the moment. Four feet high, with the appearance – and I know I'm hurting no one by saying this – of an up-turned floor mop. *Yucca elephantipes*. So named, I assume, because the woody trunk suggests the emaciated leg of a midget elephant. She – all plants are female, obviously – is not a perfect specimen (two tatty fronds, as if a cat's taken passing exception to her) but I am drawing her as if she were. I am contracted to draw 'yucca'. Not this particular yucca, with all her blemishes. Now, could I do this with Juliet? No. Juliet is Juliet. It is precisely Juliet's unique peculiarities that make her Juliet. The yucca-ness of my friend here, on the other hand, is independent of such things. Her individual characteristics are irrelevant.

OK, I anticipate Juliet's objection. I'm not comparing like with like. The equivalent to 'yucca', as a generic, I suppose, should be 'human'. But try drawing a human, in the same detail I draw my yuccas. Does it end up simply 'human'? Does it hell. It ends up old, young, male, female, fat, slim, fair, dark. A unique, if literally sketchy, individual. There is no such thing, pictorially, as simply 'human'. Moreover, this individual, drawn with only cursory detail, wears an expression. Happy, sad, angry, contrite, bored, excited. Decisions, decisions. You wonder why I prefer drawing plants?

Juliet's women friends assume I must have painted or drawn her. He's an artist, is he? they say – giving me, if I'm present, a look half appraising (so that's an artist) half, well, arch, as if at any moment I might do something rampantly unconventional, possibly of a sexual nature. "So," they murmur, "where are the pictures of you?" "Nowhere," Juliet replies, stiffly. The stiffness suggests that the admission, in a small way, humiliates her. Thus it is, undoubtedly, a criticism of me.

Would a plumber plumb the home of his girlfriend? A mechanic service her car? An architect design her house? Hell – I'm exampling myself into a corner; the answer's probably yes. Ah, but no. The trades are different, aren't they? How many ways are there of fixing a tap washer? Afterwards, the tap either drips, or it doesn't. Same with an engine – it runs sweet, or it doesn't. And the design of a house, well, no one would design a house for a girlfriend without consulting her, finding out what she wants. It would be a shared project, his execution moulded by her needs and desires.

While a portrait. It would be *for* her, but with no input *from* her, except as subject matter. Portraits express the artist's view of the subject, not the subject's view of themselves. And here, we're getting to the crunch. She wants my view of her. I don't want to give it to her.

Well, got there in the end. Forget all the tosh. We're good at making everything their fault, aren't we? The fact is that if I paint her portrait – a proper portrait, not a camera-snap equivalent – I will be revealing myself to her – myself, vis-a-vis her – and this I balk at.

I have told her. An attempt at honesty. The reason I won't

paint your portrait, I say, is because, if I do it properly, I would be exposing myself to you (don't snigger) with no reciprocation. And, I add, (on thinner ice now, but mere exposure doesn't seem enough) what I revealed would, in all probability, be scoffed at by you. I'd be making myself vulnerable. The old boy-girl thing. Loin-girding approach by boy, castrating rejection by girl.

"For God's sake," she says, rolling her eyes. "Don't be ridiculous."

"No," I say firmly. "It's you who's ridiculous. There is no guarantee you'd like it. It might even offend you."

This is a mistake. The thin ice shatters. "Since when," she hisses, "did offending me worry you? And when have I ever, ever scorned your work?" She exits violently, frightening the door. It shakes for several seconds. But she returns later, much calmer. "What I'd really appreciate,' she says, in a quiet, reasonable voice, 'is the mere fact that you'd painted my portrait. That's more important to me than what the picture looks like."

"Good heavens," I say. "Really? So you wouldn't need to see it? I could just slap the paint around, prove I've done it, and then hide it away somewhere?"

She smiles tolerantly. What a joker. Explains that of course she'd want to see it. She's just promising that she'll be nice about it. Take into account its existence, the work that went into it, as well as its actual appearance.

Terrific. So now she's saying that she will want to see the picture, and will absorb the information it conveys (because how can she not?) but will keep any response to this, tactfully, to herself. What an offer. Not only will she be privy to my true, artistically expressed feelings about her, but her reaction to these feelings will remain under wraps. How can I refuse?

"Anyway," she cajoles, "what will be so revealing about the portrait? What have you got to hide?"

This is a very intelligent question. Juliet – contrary to any impression I might have given – is very intelligent. Another way in which she differs from plants. The answer, of course, is that I don't know – I can't know – until I paint the portrait. Like any act of creation, it is a process with an unknown end. Not totally unknown – it will, at least in my own mind, centre on Juliet, or some vital aspect of her – or, indeed, us – but how, exactly, remains to be seen. After all, if you knew what the end-product of a creative work was going to be, why bother with the toil of getting there?

This interests her. (I have foolishly argued my case aloud.) A voyage of discovery. "Yeah," I say. "Me voyaging, you discovering."

"You discovering too," she cries, "and so what?' She is pink with frustration. (Quite an interesting pink, traces of carmine.) "It's not a contest," she says. "Who can hide most from whom. We're meant to be in love."

This is true. We are. Meant to be. OK, I say. I have a problem. I admit it freely. Us problematic males do. You females can lay your hopes and fears and needs and desires on the slab for anyone to pick over, but we blokes value our privacy. We are mysterious creatures, even to ourselves, and that's how we like it.

"Aha!" she cries. "Aha! So it's not *my* reaction to a portrait that's stopping you, it's *yours*."

For a moment I am dumbfounded. "I didn't say that," I mutter.

"Yes, you did," she retorts.

See, you don't get this with yuccas. They don't tire your brain. Answer back. Provoke you into saying things that may or may not be true.

OK, I say finally, because I refuse to be drawn into further argument. God knows where it'll end. Capitulate now. You win. I'll do it. She claps her hands. I have delighted her, and that's a nice feeling. Extraordinarily nice. I hadn't anticipated that. But there are rules, I say sternly. She nods. Anything, anything. Anything, eh? Wickedness tempts, but a carte blanche forces responsibility. Why am I so mature, dammit? So here they are: all reasonable rules. First: no looking till it's finished. Nod nod nod. She expected that. Understands I can't work with eyes over my shoulder. Especially not hers. Second: no enquiries over progress. No "how's it going?" even. Nod nod nod. Oh those bright, forget-me-not eyes. Third and last: no demands for explanation when it's over. The picture must be enough. I'm a visual artist. If I wanted to explain myself verbally, I'd be something else.

We are agreed. We have set aside time. I'm nervous, but it's a stewing nervousness, not unpleasant. It promises a result. First, the sketches. This is the part I particularly don't want her to see, or comment on, because it can stop me dead. I'm good at sketching. It's what I do, if I'm honest, when I draw my plants. It's all they want. A clear, painted-in sketch. She'd like these sketches of mine. If I painted one in, that would probably be enough. For her, that is. But if I'm going to do this at all, let's do it properly. Let's do it for me. Sketches are just the starting point.

It's the hand moving that stimulates the brain. When the hand is free, experimental, unrestrained. No way of knowing which way to go until I've roughed it out, seen it. Recognised it. Takes a lot of sketches, but she's being patient. And, I have to admit, she's a lovely subject to draw. My hand feels comfortable. Doesn't dither. Seems to know intuitively where to go.

Right. I've decided on a whole body portrait. I've tried heads, and head and shoulders, but they all look decapitated. Partial. I need the whole of her. And I don't want background detail. Nothing that suggests a setting. Juliet does not belong anywhere. She is just Juliet. So. Standing? Sitting? Lying? Naked? Clothed?

She has a green dress I keep getting flashes of. A soft sheath dress, clingy t-shirt material. I've asked her to put it on, and it looks kind of right. But only kind of. Nakedness appeals too, though not for the obvious reasons. Not even because it suggests intimacy. And not even because I can see she likes the idea. Wanton woman – the point of this is to satisfy me, not indulge her. But she does look good naked. Confident, natural.

I'll start with nakedness, see how it runs. I can always overpaint. I need her standing, legs together. Weight on one hip if she wants to. As long as she's upright, and doesn't give me daylight between her thighs. She's tall and slim. Lying or sitting you wouldn't see it, and tall and slim is her. Her for me, that is.

Well, I've got a general painty outline, and even the brush strokes to go with it, but her middle section is proving a problem. Her breasts, particularly. Not sure why, but they are. Bloody things. Too substantial. Too fleshy. Too animal. I need lightness, less solidity.

But I'm going to enjoy the hair. Wild red hair. Pile on the henna, I've told her.

Shit. Something isn't working. Stand back. It's not right. Juliet can see my face.

"Problems?" she says, deeply sympathetic. She's been a dream since I started doing this, no criticism, nothing's too much trouble. A revelation.

"Shut up," I reply. "I'm thinking."

She's not offended. Not remotely. She's flattered. All this wrestling concentration, over her. Except it isn't, of course. It's over me.

It's no good. Start again. I repaint the canvas. Green. The entire thing. A plain green canvas. And for a terrible few hours that's where I want to leave it. As if the colour says it all. She would be appalled, but that's not my consideration. I am appalled at myself. It shows a lack of complexity. A mental laziness, even.

Face it, I am a lazy bugger. It's years since I've done this. Years of sketching plants, painting them in, no effort at all. Story of my life. Yes, the story of my life.

Dim, too. I say it to myself, hear it in my ears, and still take hours to grasp it. The green is right. But as background. It's where she comes from.

Yes! Got it. Got it. Christ, I even understand it. No, wait, it rings bells. It's been done before. Hell. But does that matter? Think, think. No. It's OK. The reference works. The image is right. If I can capture it.

Juliet is delighted with my attitude. My commitment. This is a side of me, she says, she has been longing to see. A true artist. When not fighting with the painting I am distracted and monosyllabic; I can't think what she finds attractive about this, but there's no accounting for female taste. I am slightly proud of myself, though. I do feel committed. And, dammit, I am enjoying myself. Who'd have thought it?

I've put as much green as I can get away with into her skin tone. She's got to be distinct from the background, but connected to it. As if she has *emerged* from it. I think it works. I've solved the breast problem. I was getting hung up on what they actually looked like, rather than what I felt about them, and her. A change of perspective, that's all it took. Now there they are: as fragile, blow-in-the-breeze as the rest of her. Not that I see women's flesh as fragile, you understand – anything but – but fragile it has to be.

Fragility suggests all the right things: preciousness, perfection, the sense of something caught between too-soon (sturdily immature) and too-late (wilted, overblown). It means extraordinary, undeserved luck.

Good God. Listen to me. Sentimental fool.

Now I'm buzzing. This is right right right. All those years of practice, and I'm within tendrils of the end. I am reassured, pathetically, by the fact that Juliet will never know my journey here. Silly me; of course I'm safe. She thinks I've been at the point I've just discovered for months, and she'll never know otherwise.

She was absolutely right, too, about the act of painting being more important than the final appearance, though not in the way she meant. She was thinking about herself, not me.

There we are. Complete. Perfect. The image, necessarily, is more abstract than Juliet might have wished, but it's right, and that's what matters. She'll recognise herself. I haven't played around with her face; it's unmistakably her. Doing that didn't even feel like a concession. In fact it felt essential. Ambiguity about her identity would be a cop-out.

Stand back from it. Look at those hands. An *Amaranthus* would be jealous. And the burnished hair – eat your heart out, *Acer Purpurea*. Glad I chose lily rather than orchid between her legs. Orchid's more genital but too obvious, and lily's more approachable, and just as sexy. My Woman of Flowers. The original, if you remember your folk tales, was a lady specially created to partner some poor sod cursed never to have a mortal wife. She was unfaithful to him and in the end conspired to kill him. Well, yes. Women aren't floral Lego. Take one on, and they can hurt you.

Wonder if Juliet knows the story? Maybe, maybe not. I'll show it to her now. But no explanations. I warned her.

Glenda Beagan
The Great Master of Ecstasy

Not *that* kind of ecstasy?

No?

No. Definitely not. It's not necessary.

I sit at the little table by the skylight. It's brilliant up here in the clouds. Well that's a bit of an exaggeration I suppose. Clouds. More like chimney pots and aerials. Kieran tells me to use words properly, weighing each one like a precious stone.

Have you never taken anything, then?

Years ago I tried this and that. Had a couple of bad trips. Some people need stuff to get out of their heads.

And you don't?

I can be wherever I want to be.

You make it sound easy.

Kieran just smiles. I shut up. I must be bothering him with all this chat, and I'm frightened he'll send me away. Though I don't think he will. He never has. He's so patient. Now as I sit here watching him sketching, it's as if I hear his mind hushing me. I'm glad to know my chat doesn't bother him. And I know why it doesn't. He's centred. He hasn't got a monkey mind like the rest of us. His is a deep, quiet well. So, although he makes it sound so easy, I know it isn't. I know how many years he's studied. How many masters he's sat at the feet of, though when I said that to him he just laughed and said he'd never sit at the feet of anyone. Anyway he's a proper shaman now. People consult him. He hires a room in the Yoga Centre, Wednesdays and Saturday mornings.

I found this definition of shaman in a book about Native American tribal lore. Quoting Mircea Eliade.(I thought that was the name of a woman!) It said that the term shaman refers to 'the great master of ecstasy.'

I loved that. Even the sound of it gave me a buzz. I said it to myself over and over. The book went on to say that the shaman, 'specializes in a trance during which his soul is believed to leave his body and ascend to the sky or descend to the underworld.'

And I know that when Kieran says he can be wherever he wants to be, he means exactly what he says.

His flat is weird but it's got a good feeling to it. It's on the fourth floor. In the attics. The ceilings slope and all the windows are skylights. There are no blinds so, at night, with the house being so tall, high above most of that orangey town glow, you can lie in your bed and swim in the moonlight. That's what it feels like. Now I've got my own place I'm never here at night which is a shame because I loved that feeling of being way up in the sky among the stars. At the time of the full moon her face seems to peer right down at you, just above your head. I always think of the moon as a she.

The first time I came to the flat was when Kieran rescued me. That sounds a bit dramatic but it's true. I'd been sleeping rough all summer which wasn't bad, in fact I liked it. I found good places, one was on what's left of the dunes behind the lifeboat station, and the other was in the

Jubilee Gardens. When they were closing I'd make sure I was well out of it, hiding by the incinerator thing next to all those greenhouses at the back.

But winter came all at once and it was a different story then. I don't want to talk about the way I was when Kieran found me, or what I'd been doing just to keep going. I owe him a lot.

I was really ill. I had bronchitis and pleurisy. And I'd got this skin infection, with my skin kind of all peeling and wet. Kieran isn't into doctors, not ordinary doctors, but he knows herbalists and people like that. He got me eating properly for the first time in years. Then, nearly three months later, he got me to write to my parents, just to say I was still alive. He was going to Manchester to take part in a sweat lodge and he posted the letter there. I made him promise. I knew that if my parents had any idea where I was they'd come looking for me, so the letter just had to be posted somewhere far enough away. Even then I didn't trust him completely. I can't believe that after all he'd done for me I still had my doubts. I was afraid he'd get in touch with them. I grabbed his hands and looked up into his eyes to read them.

All I saw was honesty.

From the skylight in the little living-room/kitchen you can see across the rooftops to the hills. They look blue and gentle. Sometimes misted, like a Chinese painting, sometimes sharp and clear. You get this illusion that they're so close you could reach out and touch them.

And then there's the top of the Catholic Church like a great shark's fin.

Wow, I said, Jaws. Just look at that!

This was the first time I'd felt strong enough to stand and peer out of the skylight without being propped up.

Stupidly, like a big kid, I started to mimic the music

from the film – DUH DUH, DUH DUH, DUH DUH, DUH DUH.

It's good to see you can be silly, Kieran said.

When I was able to get out a bit I found the church, Our Lady of the Assumption. It's opposite the Yoga Centre. Sometimes on Wednesdays when Kieran was there doing his consultations I'd get really bored and restless in the flat. I'd go and wait for him outside, sitting in that little Zen garden, all raked gravel and stones. I'd rake that gravel myself, for something to do, and I got to like it, the way all the rippling lines formed in those whitish little stones, like lines on the sand when the tide's gone out. The rake was wood, all wood, even the teeth of it, and these were widely spaced specially to make the right patterns.

If it rained I'd go and sit in the church. It was a modern building, a peculiar shape from the outside, like a wonky pyramid, and it was the topmost tip of this that you could see looking like a shark's fin from Kieran's window. I'd turn round there on the pavement and look up over the roofs to see if I could make out which was his flat. I couldn't be sure, though. Thee were so many houses that looked all the same, tall and kind of grand originally, I should think, when they were all boarding houses and people hadn't heard of the Costa Brava. Or Florida. Now all these houses are multiple lets. There's lots of druggies.

Kieran say he doesn't pay much rent for his place partly because of the street it's in, which has got a bad reputation (even us dossers had heard it was a place to keep clear of) and partly because it's right at the top of the building, with those funny wedge shaped rooms. But it's exactly these things that make the place special, and Kieran has got it so nice, all painted white with lots of trailing ivies and ferns in glass bells. And on the skylights he's hung pendants on leather thongs. They work like mobiles, all different shapes and colours, with silver edges and silver spirals on them.

The spiral is a sacred shape. Kieran's shown me pictures of this great grave stone at Newgrange in Ireland, and it's covered with spirals. The place is so old it's even older than Stonehenge. I'd love to go there.

Kieran does a lot of sketching. He calls them his preliminaries. He gets the idea of people's totem animals from their consultations with him. I know he doesn't charge people much for these sessions, only what he thinks they can afford, but he does make quite a bit of money from his artwork. sometimes. He gets commissions and he says it's surprising how many people have owl totems. The way he paints then they're all different. They're magic. They don't look as if they're painted at all and they don't look as if they're on a flat surface either. You feel you could touch the feathers, and they'd be real feathers. You feel those owls could rise up out of their frames and fly.

Once he painted a special commission for an American. He was a financier or something. I asked Kieran how on earth he'd got to know this bloke who was rolling in money. Apparently he'd seen Kieran's advertisement somewhere. I didn't know he advertised.

You won't find my ads in magazines in the corner shop, he said. They're in specialist journals.

I teased him then for sounding dead stuck-up and posh! But it also made me realise there was another aspect to Kieran, one I didn't know anything about. Anyway this painting was completed but the man never turned up. I'd have been very angry, all that wasted time and energy. Kieran wasn't. He said there must be a reason. I got the feeling he somehow knew that the man was dead.

You could sell it to someone else, I said. It's beautiful.

Kieran shook his head. He set the painting up on the mantelpiece. It was of a pair of elf owls on a cactus. These are the tiniest owls you could imagine, very pretty with big golden eyes. In the painting the cactus has a hole in its side where one of the owls is peeping out. It's obvious its nest is there, right inside. The flesh of the cactus itself is a yellowy green, ridged and rather blotchy but one section of it is ablaze with flowers. These are almost as big as the owls themselves, like sunflowers, with crowns of white petals and yellow middles.

Did he describe them to you or did you have a picture to work from? I asked him.

As soon as he told me what he wanted I imagined how they were, he said. Kieran is often matter-of-fact and mysterious at the same time.

When I was ill I slept in Kieran's bed and somehow he managed to sleep on the thin lumpy sofa in the other room. The bedroom skylight looked out towards the sea and although you couldn't see it, what with all the buildings in between, you knew it was there because the light was different, brighter and whiter. I think it was being with Kieran that made me notice things like this. I'm sure I never used to. Now I saw things, really saw things. I saw the shine on the top rim of the Big Wheel on the horizon, and on a clear evening when the wind was blowing the right way, I could hear the far squeals and howls of the Ghost Train. And I watched the gulls do their aerial acrobatics. Before, when I'd heard all their squawkings, it was all just a noise to me. It got on my nerves. Now it seemed there was a kind of music in it, and this music had moods. Sad, happy, pensive. I was sensitive to everything around me, everything I touched. Everything that touched me. When I told Kieran about this he said it was because I'd been so ill. Now it was like everything was new.

I admit that once I was better I expected him to sleep with me. I took it for granted he would. I mean, I'm not ugly or anything. But he wasn't interested. I felt rejected. I wanted to say thank you for all he'd done for me and what else had I got to give him? I began to think he was gay or something.

I had so much to learn.

But once I was better, really better, he suggested I look for a place of my own. He also got me to see the DSS. people so I could get some benefit. I felt guilty. He'd fed me all this time and had never asked for a penny. I'd never really thought about what it was costing him.

The problem I had with you was getting you to eat in the first place, he said.

Even when I got my own bedsit and started on a back to work course at the tech, (I.T. and Business Admin) I still went to see him. I was nervous at first. Yes, he'd got me well again, got me back on my feet, but perhaps he wouldn't want to see me anymore.

He did though. Who needs that other kind of ecstasy?

Things changed now. It wasn't like I was dependent, the way I had been. We were more sort of equal, though how could anybody be equal with Kieran? Now we talked about what he believed in, what being a shaman was all about. He was teaching me, only it wasn't like being taught. With Kieran I just absorbed information. I learned about the Lakota Sioux medicine man he'd worked with. I learned about Taoism and the Aborigine Dreamtime. Then there was Cuchulain, the Hound of Ulster, and Finn. All those Irish heroes. I learned about the Matter of Britain, about runes and rituals and the great web of wyrd, about the guardian skulls Kieran had seen lodged in the chimney breasts of old farms, and the spirit lore that went with them. He recited a wonderful poem to me that gave me shivers down my spine, composed by a linguist in Russia who was trying to discover an ancient language that once all people shared. His name was Illich-Svitych. He called the language Nostratic.

Language
is a ford
through
the river of time;

to the house
of those who are gone
it leads us.

But there
he shall not go
who is afraid of deep water....

Kieran knew this poem off by heart. I wrote it down with
a biro on the back of my hand.

Before I did so, I rolled up my sleeves. There were all
the scars, no longer a livid red but still furrowed, like tram-
lines up my arms. It was as if another person had inflicted
those injuries, not me. I'd started cutting when I was just
turned fourteen. I'd stopped when I ran away from home.
Kieran never asked me about the cutting. I think he knew
I couldn't give him a reason for why I needed to do it. Lots
of bits of reasons, maybe. All I did know for sure was that
I'd never need to do it again.

I always believed that when you were dead you were dead.
Finished. End of story. I don't now.

I remember it all as if it was a bad dream. Not real. Jon
and Vanda from the Yoga Centre came round to tell me.
It was early morning. They'd found him in the garden
when they went to open up and he must have been lying
there overnight, he'd lost so much blood. Some people
must have gone for him after he'd finished his consultations. Thought he had a lot of money on him, druggies I
suppose. We reckon there must have been at least two of

them and that they must have been waiting for him

I couldn't understand how anyone could hurt Kieran. I sat by his bed in the hospital, listening to the ventilator breathing for him, looking at all those tubes. Already I felt he wasn't there, that this was just his shell. I knew it was just a matter of time before they switched off that machine.

The landlord asked me to clear Kieran's flat. I sat there in the half dark, thinking about him, looking at his painting of the elf owls. Then, as I watched, they seemed to glow, even move a little. The pendants on the skylights tingled. The spiral shapes shone on the walls around, shone and danced and circled, then all those ivies and ferns, their shadows. Everything seemed to be dancing. A warm bright wind seemed suddenly to be blowing through the room, with, just for a second or two, a quick shift of light in the painting. I don't care if you don't believe me. I don't expect you to, but for just a moment I felt an owl alight on my shoulder. I felt its feathers, its little cold hard beak touching my face.

Roger Granelli
Disturbing the Peace

The crowd surged past Elkins' window. A beast with snarling, jagged edges. Two youths fell into his garden, bouncing over the top of his privet hedge. They laughed and shook cans of beer, using them like miniature fire extinguishers to squirt each other. Elkins ducked behind his curtains as eyes probed his window. As one, the youths unzipped their tight jeans and urinated against his door. Animals marking out a territory. Elkins flattened himself against a wall and squinted through the gap in the curtain.

He had not seen the crowd detach into individuals before. No-one had ever been this close. That they might try to enter. An old, cold sweat came back, terrible and familiar. Touching his soul with ice. But the youths were called by others and went lurching out through the front gate to join the throng. The noise peaked now, a strenuous exercising of lungs without any apparent connection to thought. Elkins knew this, too.

Wales, Walia, had been all but unknown to him in 1946. Just the briefest of references in his Cracow schoolbooks. A dirty, industrialised part of Britain, linguistically bizarre. It had been alien then, but safe. So safe. Cardiff a city that was adjusting to the anti-climax of victory and the knowledge that problematic lives would roll back into place once more.

The Jewish community placed him with Gold, a jeweller. Some years later he achieved his own modest shop. In the docks that still bustled then he created an oasis of calm, symbolised by the stuffed and glazed tortoise he placed in his window. Raised on a plinth that rotated slowly. He built a clock into the base of the plinth. The tortoise's regular and orderly marking of time became his trademark. His new life.

The match was in progress. He heard the swell of massed voices, baiting, cajoling, threatening. They shouted for a game but he heard Berlin. Munich. And saw the gates of Oswiecim closing on him as he trudged through them with the others from the train. Cotton wool clouds in a cobalt blue sky. Mahler's Fifth playing through crackling speakers. The gate's welcoming words. A welcome to hell. And that smell, an acrid infestation of the nostrils as he received his filthy, dead man's pyjamas. The whimpers that began around him.

Elkins still had the clock. The tortoise was still now but it was his memento, a last minute salvage of a closing business. He gave the chrome plinth a quick polish and caught a clouded image of himself. A long, thin face and red-rimmed eyes framed by wire glasses. What was left of his hair a fine silver. Skin chalky from a life indoors. A prison pallor. Add a skull cap, intensify the eyes and elongate the stubble of his chin beard and you had every caricature that had lived down the ages. The demons of Nazi films.

He creaked as he sat down. His bones hurt increasingly, the limp in his left leg becoming more prominent. He compared himself with the rippling power he'd seen in the garden. Hopeless.

Kev's voice was hoarse. City had lost again. Wankers. He had shouted off the effects of the morning's beer and wanted more. Waiting for Dean to catch up with him he leant against the wall of the pub and spat into the road. Sending out a series of wet projectiles, each one travelling a little further. His wiry frame wore the blue shirt of his team, and the regulation high, laced-up boots. Weapons on both feet. Hair was cropped so close to his head it looked like shadow. Each arm was tattooed. Dean had them all over but Kev didn't fancy that. Dean was a stupid bastard, but good in a rumble. Kev ached for a bit of violence, but it was getting harder, with the pigs kitted up with their fucking videos and the like. Dean appeared.

'You getting 'em in or what,' Kev said, 'I'm fucking skint.'

They crashed into the pub, to be saluted by their mates. The pub was a fortress. Ragged decor, sepia photographs of old wars on its walls, and a floor covering that did not want to release the feet of drinkers. Beer came in plastic glasses.

'Did you see that geezer in that poxy flat?' Kev muttered.

'What geezer?'

'Where we had that slash. He thought I couldn't see his mug behind that curtain. Sad old git, he was. I hate 'em. Should be put down before they get that sad.'

'Shuffling old bastards,' Dean added.

He liked to add phrases of support to Kev's sentences, so he could share in the glory of his words. His pint lasted two swallows and he split it down the side when he banged the empty plastic onto the bar. Twenty of Kev's disciples laughed and began to chant.

Kev's crowd adopted the fortress as their summer watering hole. They were there the last Saturday of May. City had gone down and the action had cooled.

'What we doing this summer then, Kev?' a voice asked.

'Dunno what you lot are doing but I'm going nicking again. I've had a gutsfull of being skint. That giro is only good for one night's piss-up.'

'We doing cars again, Kev?' Dean asked.

'Cars be fucked. Nah, that's yesterday, that is. Every bugger's got a radio.'

'What then?'

'Houses innit. Got to be. And shops maybe. We don' need nothing to ramraid 'em with. We can use Deano.'

He turned to the long table of faces, which laughed on cue. He left the table and took Dean into a corner.

'Listen, you was from round here, before you come on the estate. What's the crack?'

Dean looked at him blankly.

'Jesus wept,' Kev muttered, 'I forget how thick you are sometimes.'

He tapped Dean's head and pretended to look inside his ear. Dean grinned.

'This place used to be posh years ago,' Kev said. 'Maybe there's a few of the fuckers left, sitting on their notes.'

'There's pensioners, like, down them flats by the ground.'

Kev thought back a few weeks.

'Aye, that old sod in the window. Nah, he looked piss-poor. Gemme a pint.'

Kev went out to the pub's entrance. He liked to stand in the doorway when there was a bit of sun. And feel like he owned something. By the time he was twenty he had given up on work. Why not, it had given up on him. At twenty three he was the oldest in the group and his worn, pinched face already turning its back on its youth. He looked as if he had been born with the blue smudges under his eyes.

Kev looked down the street to the flats. At least they would have videos, which were good for fifty bucks. Dean brought out the beer, sloshing some of it on the pavement.

An old geezer was coming down the road on the other side. Kev stared across at the man and spat into the street. The man had an overcoat on, something that had been expensive once. The old man gave no sign that he was aware of him. He tried to fade into the road as he passed on quickly, limping on his left side, his eyes stuck to the floor like eggs to a pan. Old bugger's afraid of me, Kev thought, with a touch of pride. If it had been dark he might have considered a mugging. There was something about the old git. Fuck aye. From that flat down the road. He followed him down to it with his eyes to make sure.

'We going to town, or what?' Dean asked.

'Aye, might as well. But we'll be back down here later.'

Elkins had not expected the youth to be there, now that the football season was over. He avoided looking at him, in a way he had learned so well it was etched on his character. Unseeing eyes had been his one defence. The ability to never look at any of them unless it was absolutely vital. When it had been he'd willed his eyes to melt into nothingness, and say that their owner was not worth bothering about. His turn could come later. Anytime. It was humility taken to its ultimate extreme allied to his youth. He was able to work on whilst others dropped. Living off his usefulness. Doing what was necessary to survive at Oswiecim. The world called it by its German name now.

He had been to the post office to send letters. Letters kept him going, made the course of his life a little easier. He wrote to three people, Krygiel, in New York, Kowalski in Tel Aviv and Rita Bloom, who had arrived at the camp in the last few weeks and had been overlooked in that last rush of murder. Rita was the only one of them who had managed to integrate. Living in Manchester, where she had raised a large family.

He played chess with Krygiel. The professor had beaten him just twice in forty years. When he played chess he entered the game, immersed himself in its strategies and saw the routes to victory with a confidence he could not countenance in real life. Take it up, Krygiel had urged. People make money at it now, lots of money. But he never did. Never could.

Kev drank what money Dean had. Beer was a problem. The more he drank the more he could take. It cost a lot to get pissed. He had only had six pints, but it was enough to make him feel meaner than usual. To hate his poverty and the world that kept him poor.

'Come on brain-dead,' Kev said, 'let's go back down the fortress. This place sucks.'

Dean followed Kev across town.

'How much you got left?' Kev asked.

Dean held out a hand with assorted coins in its palm.

'Less than a quid. Jesus Christ, that settles it. I'm going down the road tonight, down them flats.'

'What we gonna do, Kev?'

'You ain't gonna do nothing 'cept keep a look out. And sort anyone out that needs it. We'll try that old sod with the coat first. Get his video and sell it on the estate in the morning.'

'How much we'll get?'

Kev thought for a moment.

'Thirty quid. You can have half.'

They hung around the pub as long as they could, then walked down the street when it had emptied of drinkers. Kev sauntered, pushing back his shoulders and grinding his hands in his pockets. Dean padded along at his side. His human Rottweiler. Kev felt like someone again.

Kev's malevolent stare had disturbed Elkins. A catalyst to

spark another cycle of recall, in what had been a year of deadly anniversaries. First: Auschwitz, then Belsen. Others would follow, a chronology he found hard to deal with. The massed candles on the railway tracks, his tracks, had moved him, but also stripped naked his guilt. That he had survived into another world, that he had wanted to. A world that had learned little.

Sweat formed on his brow. He was up late but did not want to sleep. Reactivated nightmares dwelt there. Always the last days, the frenetic but uncrazy killing, when they no longer cared if the living were crammed into the ovens. And the end that did not seem possible. His eighty wasted pounds twitching in the unnatural quiet of abandonment. Hearing a bird call as it flew overhead, but not sure if this was a last trick of hell, and that zycie, life, would still be taken from him. Waking with a sigh too tired and knowing to ever be a scream.

'Don' stop, you stupid sod,' Kev hissed.

He nudged Dean past Elkins' flat

'Looks like there's a back lane,' he said. 'We'll go round there. It'll be easier'

They waited in the shadows until all the lights went off in the flats. Kev pushed open Elkins' back gate.

'Fucking rotten, that is,' he muttered.

Kev's approach was direct. A piece of housebrick wrapped in Dean's jacket shattered the glass square on the back door of the flat. Kev reached inside to find the key in the lock.

'Stupid old buggers. They never learn.'

Elkins heard the glass breaking. He had almost expected it. There was something about this night. His curtains were open and streetlight illuminated his chessboard. He had moved a knight to accommodate Krygiel but had not yet responded.

They did not see him at first, as they fumbled their way into the room.

'There's nuffink here,' Dean said, 'I can't even see no telly'

'Shut the curtains and put the light on,' Kev whispered. Dean jumped slightly when he saw the tortoise. His groping hands probed Elkins' tenebrous corner and connected with his face.

'Jesus Christ, there's someone there.'

Light flooded the room as Kev found the switch.

'Well, well,' Kev said, 'it's grandad. Sat all alone in the dark. We come to visit you like. Don' want no trouble do you? Nah, course you don't.'

Dean was confused. His fists ached to take over from his meagre thought processes but the old man looked pathetic. Kind of shrivelled, somehow.

'I reckon you're cracked, Pop,' Kev said.

He looked around the room and saw that Dean was right. No telly, video, no fucking nothing except books and a clapped out looking radio.

'Ain't nothing here,' Dean repeated.

'I can see that, piss-brain.'

Kev brushed a row of books from the top shelf of a case. They tumbled to the floor in a shower of dust.

'Where d'you keep it then?' he shouted.

He pushed his face close to Elkins, showering him with beer-breath spittle. Elkins saw the snarl of his imperfect teeth and found his voice.

'If it's money you want I have very little,' he said.

'You foreign or summat?'

Kev squinted at him more closely.

'I know you. You're the old git with that poxy place down the docks. My old woman used to go there. You're a Yid.'

Yyd, a word from the old country. Elkins looked through a thousand Kevs to the past.

'Not paying attention, Pop.'

A stinging blow jerked his head back. Kev turned to Dean.

'We've struck lucky here, kid. He must be loaded and don' spend much by the look of this dump.'

'He ain't got no telly,' Dean said.

'I'll ask you one more time,' Kev said. 'I know you bastards, you'll have it stashed somewhere, away from the fucking taxman.'

He grabbed Elkins by his lapel, and pulled him up.

'Now look, you don't want no more. See this boy here, this big bastard, he ain't right, see. And once he starts.'

'I tell the truth,' Elkins said. 'I have just a few pounds in my purse.'

He handed this to Kev, who snatched it, opened it and counted out the coins.

'Eight fucking quid. You must be joking. Listen, this one is thick, I ain't.'

Kev's hand worked across Elkins' face a few more times. He tasted blood inside his mouth. Its old, familiar salt.

'Watch him,' Kev said, 'I'm gonna have a look round.'

He rifled his way through the flat, rubbishing things quietly. No money.

It was a long five minutes. Elkins knew that when Kev returned from his fruitless search rage would be reinforced by frustration, to create a legitimate grievance in the young man's mind. He would he diminished into a vile speck, a thing to prey on and abuse. Then Kev's actions would not only be necessary, they would be justified. Dean looked at the chessboard.

'Wassis?'

'Only a game.'

Dean picked up a queen, and twirled her carved wood in his great hands.

'Fuck off,' he said, 'them's ornaments.'

But he replaced the queen, quite gently.

'Tell him where the money is,' he murmured.

Elkins saw that this bovine one was not innately danger-
ous. Men like him had abounded in the camp, the fodder
of the small and mean. Something cold pressed against his
leg. The paper knife he'd used earlier, the one Krygiel had
sent him. A thin but strong blade with the Star of David
on the handle. Kev re-entered the room.

'I can't find fuck all,' he said

'It is how I told you,' Elkins said. 'You have picked the
wrong one.'

'Don' you make a fool out of me, you old sod. I *know*
there's money here.'

'You are too late, my young friend. Yes, I did have
money, but I gave it away. To Israel.'

'Who the fuck's he?' Dean asked.

'Israel is a country.'

'What's he on about, Kev?''

'Shut up, you donkey,' Kev tugged at Dean. 'An' you
used my name, I've told you about that.'

'Oh yeah, sorry Kev.'

It was getting out of control. Kev knew he was losing it.
The blurring of his eyes. The irresistible urge to go apeshit.

'Go on, then,' Kev shouted, 'do him. Do the fucker!'

Dean was confused, and did not move.

'But he's old, though,' he muttered.

'For fucksake,' Kev yelled, 'Why do I bother? I'll do him
myself. Come here, you old bastard.'

He jerked Elkins to his feet, lined up his face for pound-
ing and received the paper knife between the ribs.

Elkins was amazed at its ease of entry. There was a
hiatus of silence, a crushing moment which made him think
there had never been noise. Kev's body seemed frozen, his
face locked with shock. Then he dropped down, emitting
one small gasp and the word 'fuck.'

'What you done?' Dean cried, 'What you done to my mate?' He stepped towards Elkins, looked down at Kev, at the red escaping from him, then back again to Elkins. It was too much for him. He crashed out of the flat, straight into the arms of the police. Called by Elkins' neighbour.

He still had the knife in his hand when the police entered. They prised it away from him. Carefully.

'Looks like the old fella flipped,' an officer said.

They cordoned off the flat and waited for CID. A sergeant arrived. He looked at Kev. At his dead staring eyes.

'Kevin Carl Jenkins' he muttered. He turned to Elkins. 'Want to tell us what happened, sir?'

Elkins looked out of the window. At the sky soaked with the orange of the street lights. He felt calm. So very calm. An absence of fear. For the first time. Perhaps this is what calm means, he thought.

'I fought back,' he said quietly.

Babs Horton
Colouring Mother

She is colouring her mother. For this daily act of worship she uses her special paintbox. Soon holes will grow in the paint, worn thin through constant use. For mother is always painted in pastel colours. Pale pinks and lilacs, pale lemons and watery aquamarine. She has coloured her mother so many times before. These portraits are the product of her dreams, figments of her imagination. She has never seen her mother. But she knows that wherever she is, mother will be the eggshell blue of a racing sky, the pink flush of the dawn, as dusky as evening lavender. She will be white as clouds, laced with silver.

Only in her nightmares mother is painted differently. Then she is red and black. Bright blue. Green.

'Don't keep asking your father questions about your mother dear,' Aunt Lydia tells her, with a querulous and worried voice. 'It makes him see red.'

'Mentioning her name is red rag to a bull,' Nanny tells the new kitchen maid, in hushed tones.

Then she finds out that her mother has green fingers but she can't remember where she heard this or who said it.

As time passes she colours mother differently. She wears

more holes in the paint box. The pastel painted lady has green fingers. The green becomes used up. Then the black.

Black. Her mother is a black sheep. So says Aunt Lydia. And the family, those who have not gone to war, echo the same.

Her father should never have married a foreigner murmurs the household. There are holes worn in the arrays of blue in her paintbox. Blue. Blue for murder. Blue murder if you mentioned her name.

Purple and violet she never uses. For purple is the colour of the Lenten altar cloth. Purple is denial. Purple is wistful, waiting and yearning. Violet is the end of the rainbow and unattainable.

The house and the servants whisper colours. They paint a different picture of her mother.

Her father is a jealous man. Green for jealousy.

'Quite mad at times...' a scullery maid whispers.

'Black and blue. Hit her black and blue they say....'

Red. Moses parted the red sea. A great red curtain of sea. Red as blood. Crimson. Pillar box red. Blood is thicker than water.

She knows that seas separate her from mother. Buoyant seas that kiss golden shores, seas that bubble with silver fish, seas that echo mermaids' songs.

The tide changes. At the end of the War the servants are all gone. Her father lies in a field, where poppies will grow. Gone.

A child needs her mother. Aunt Lydia laments for the first time. She can't stay here shut up in the house with me....

The sea is not aquamarine or blue, or shimmering turquoise. It is black and grey, peppered with slime green veins. On the boat she lies in the cabin and the drone of the engines runs through her bones. The white hull of the ship, slices through water. Her stomach is full of water, salt seas slop in her insides until she is all sea, spewing up the sea. She drowns in salt tears until anchors and ropes tie them to a foreign shore and the pull of the English tide is too weak and tired to draw them back.

They are spilled out down the gangplanks, shoals of nervous travellers open mouthed, white around the gills.

In the car she can still smell England. She smells polish. Tobacco. Brylcreem and her father. Inside the car it is England. Outside they are in a foreign place. They pass small villages at dawn, grey against the pink wash of the early light. Yellow towns in mid-morning where the sun, browns the bread. Bread sticks that are white inside and fluffy as clouds. All around there are seas of sunflowers. High as houses. Vast yellow fields to drown in.

Up, up, to the top of the world that is blue and black with birds, past chalets where church bells and cow bells, peal away the day. There are eagles on the wing. Eagles dropping fast to earth and the car plummets hell for leather down steep tracks.

They are in a land where the sun burns on and on. There is dust and garlic on, the hot breath of the wind. There are statues in the middle of nowhere. Blue ladies abandoned in great deserts under the fierce sun, guarding jam jars of dying flowers. There are towns carved out of rock with peepholes for windows. Eyes that stare. Eyes that move. There are shutters on houses. Shutters that keep you in and shut you out.

Aunt Lydia perspires and melts on the lumpy beds of hotel rooms. Cool rooms with broken rush-backed chairs, baked plaster, like the icing on an ageing cake. Stark crucifixes, black as gangrene, dissect bare walls.

In the dust of villages there are barefoot children with winking, sloe eyes, chickens scattering, arch-backed cats on overlong legs journeying through the dust.

A lone donkey on a hill brays at the encroaching dusk.

His mouth opens and closes. Opens and closes, swallowing the ball of red hot sun until the donkey glows and the world is black.

The car stops when they reach the town where her mother lives. The world tilts on its axis, tilts them closer toward the sun. They walk, through a blinding square of light. Only the church casts a shadow. Dry mouthed gargoyles leer and stare. The sun, like a great catherine wheel, spins in the sky. Everywhere is deserted. The schoolyard that borders one end of the square is empty, desolate in its silence. There is a faint rustle above her head as the breeze poaches through the plane trees, trees that fuse with the clear Spanish sky. Aunt Lydia and the driver pore over a map. Try to decipher ornate writing on a piece of paper they have carried all the way from England. The trees stir, ruffle, bubble up, a green broth above them.

They turn into an alleyway and at once, the day becomes dusk. Behind her she sees the driver silhouetted against the light. A black gaunt figure growing smaller every second

Aunt Lydia's hand grows clammy and loosens its grasp, she tightens her own grip, in fear. Their feet make little noise on the cobbles. Houses on either side of the alley stretch up to the crack of sky. In one of these houses her mother lurks, waiting like a black spider in a cobwebby corner.

They stand before a house. Flowers bedeck this house. From floor to sky. Red splashes, orange blooms, on every window sill. Flowers stretch in terraces up to the sky. Vivid in the gloom.

Her mother has green fingers.

The door is shut. There is a bell handle which Aunt Lydia pulls, taking her hand away from her as she does so. She hugs her arms around her waist. She wants to wee. To cry, to run away back out of this alley, back into the light. To the smell of polish, of stale cigarette smoke and brylcreem.

Deep in the belly of the house the bell rings, the sound of shuffling feet approaching, old slippers on ancient legs.

The old woman who answers the door has no teeth. She is fat, and wears a black bunchy skirt, black thick socks rolled down around her ankles. She blinks in the half light. Opens her mouth. An infinity of blackness where her lips had been.

Her mother is a black sheep.

Aunt Lydia pushes her forward, a keen nudge in the small of her back. Her spine recoils, resists, but the old woman's hand comes out from the black lair of her sleeve. She is pulled over the threshold and into the web. The door closes behind her and her eyes relinquish the last of the light....

The dark and the cool pull at her with long fingers. There is light at the end of the tunnel. White light. Green light. A red splash. A garden. In the depths of this house there is a garden.

She is washed in green light. The orange splash of a fruit falling. Green and orange merge. The white froth of a fountain hurts her eyes. Gushing layers of lacy water.

There is a brown table, a decanter of wine. Red as blood. There are olives in a bowl, like dark, black eyes clustering to watch her.

Above her the sky reels, and she is down a well where footholds of windowsills climb to the sky, bright flowers point the way. Up and up.

On a balcony above her, the shutters are opening. Slowly.

The light catches its breath, floods inwards, flushing a face outwards. Hands resting on a window sill, merging with flowers. Eyes, pale green, underwater eyes. A splash of gentian violet, deepening to purple. Her eyes hurt. Red wine splashes from a glass, across the white cloth, paling to pink.

A door shudders and exhales a sigh.

She closes her eyes, keeps the light out. She smells blossom and the tang of the citrus fruit burns her eyes.

She has hair as black and blue as the raven's wing. Skin brown and soft, lips and eyes painted with too wet a brush, the eyes melting, green tears trailing. Green tears trailing down onto a gown of violet and purple....

And then the touch, the touch of mother. Like gossamer spider webs, spun with desire. Hot blood, pumps through the veins of the earth, moving like a current, bursting through arteries, jerking limbs into spasms, that merge and lock and hold and will never again let go. The laying down of a head on a damp breast, a cheek pressed to a wet head. Around them bougainvillaea hurtles from the walls, water-falls of purple profusion. They both know now that purple is not a colour, it is an emotion and that ecstasy, ecstasy is the colour of damp violets.

Caryl Ward
Wolf Man

Trevor stood in the bath and stared at himself in the full-length mirror on the wall. He must do it now. He didn't care that it meant losing his job. Katrina was all that mattered.

He ran his fingers through the hair on his face. It was fairly soft there with a sheen to it. He picked up the dress-making scissors that he had borrowed from Rosie. His hands were shaking, and his eyes looked back at him from the mirror like those of a frightened animal. He slid the blades of the scissors as close to his skin as he could and cut the hair from his forehead. He snipped carefully around his eyes, and around his long straight nose. He cut over his high cheek-bones and in the hollows beneath. He cut around his mouth then down and around his pointed chin where it was streaked with white. Holding his left ear with his left hand, he snipped carefully at the tufts growing from and behind it. Then he turned his head and, watching himself in the mirror, he cut around his right ear.

He put the scissors down on the edge of the bath and stared at himself. He hadn't seen his face as clearly as this for years and it was like looking at another person. When

Trevor was born he had been covered with a soft golden down, and as he grew older it had grown darker and coarser. When he was nineteen he had joined the travelling fair as Wolf Man.

Trevor had hated the fair at first, and had refused to mix with the other freaks. Then he became ill with a bad bout of flu, and Rosie the Fat Lady had looked after him like a mother. She had given him soup and hot drinks, and when his fever was at its worst she had stroked his hot sweaty fur with her soft sausage-like fingers. He broke down and wept; confessed that he hated the life he was leading, being in his cage for hours on end with people staring at him. The children who poked sticks through the bars and spat at him, making him cower from one side of the cage to the other, terrified him. And the old ladies who shrieked at the sight of him, and the others who threw him crusts of sandwiches and chips from their newspapers, expecting him to eat off the floor, disgusted him so much that he felt that his life was not worth living.

Rosie, who weighed 642 pounds, understood how he felt, and pulled his head onto her lap and her fat had enveloped him like a womb. She told him that he would get used to it in time, that they all hated it at first, but everyone had to earn a living somehow. And it was a good place for people like them. They were protected with the fair, it was the only place where they could be really safe.

She told him about her life before she joined the fair. She had worked in a shoe factory in Leicester and had been good at her job. Then she began to get fat very quickly. She was gaining weight at the rate of twenty pounds a week, and the other women refused to walk home with her. Then she got so heavy that she broke the stools that the factory provided for the workers, and she was forced to stand up and work. She didn't really mind that, but the union complained, and they all wanted her out, and although the managing director felt sorry for her there was nothing he could do, as by standing up she was breaking the contract set out in the working conditions. He offered her a small sum of money to get out, but Rosie knew it wouldn't last long and continued to go to work. Then one night when she had been walking home, a gang of workers had cornered her, prodding and pinching her, jeering and laughing. She had screamed loudly, and the police arrived. The workers had run away shouting that if she came into work they would get her again. She had been frightened for her life, and had joined the fair.

'We're freaks, Trev, there's no getting away from the fact,' she had said. 'We're the ones in cages – but it's them that come to look at us is the animals.'

Trevor had settled down after his talk with Rosie. He made friends with the Bearded Lady and the dancing Dwarf Quads. When he was in his cage he treated his audience like animals. He learned how to curl his lips back and snarl viciously, how to bare his teeth and bark, how to articulate a spine-chilling howl. Trevor's wolf language was a language that lay behind all language and the people tried to copy him and snarled and howled back at him. He scampered round and round his cage on all fours to amuse them. He offered to shake hands with them through the bars of his cage, and when they took his hand he would pull their hand through the bars and give it a playful, or a not so playful bite. Trevor now felt in control of his singularity and used it to demonstrate to the stupid people who came to gawp at him what they had evolved from. It wasn't such a bad life after he had come to terms with it. And after all, he was Wolf Man – which was better than being nothing.

He began to clip the hair on his chest. It was thick and coarse there, but it was easier to cut than on his face. He worked quickly, and the hair fell in black clumps into the white bath. As he snipped lower, he became more adept.

He stopped and stared at his navel. He couldn't remember ever seeing it before and had forgotten that he must have one. Cutting around his genitals was tricky; he left a few tufts and proudly fingered his new-found pubic hair.

He started on his left arm, moving up from the wrist to his shoulder. He lifted his arm above his head and cut the hair from the back of his arm. He did the same to his right arm. The scissors were awkward to use with his left hand, but he managed. He placed his left foot on the side of the bath and cut the hair on his shin and thigh, then the back of his leg and the inside of his thigh, and lastly his foot and toes. He did the same to his right leg. Then he put the scissors down on the bath between the taps.

Standing under the shower and lathering himself with soap, he wondered if Katrina would have him. She had only been with the fair for two weeks, but Trevor fell in love with her the minute he set eyes on her. Her skin was the colour of clotted cream, and her blue-black hair hung down her back to her waist. Trevor had tried to talk to her on two occasions. She was a fortune teller and he had asked her to read the cards for him.

'Shove off, Wolf Man, go and find yourself a freak,' she had said, flashing her green eyes.

He turned off the shower and his black hair swirled around and clogged the plug-hole. He scooped it up. There was enough of it to make a rug. He'd show her. He wasn't a wolf. He was a man, with a man's feelings and needs. He opened the packet of disposable razors that he'd bought that morning and lined them up on the edge of the bath. There were six. He hoped it would be enough. He hadn't shaved for almost twenty years, and then he had only done his face and hands. He had no idea how long a razor would last, or how long it would take him. It seemed a rather small object to use on such a vast area. He shaved his face first, and cut himself three times. He left two lines of stubble for eyebrows and removed the rest. He had to leave a few wisps around his ears, which were impossible to get at. His neck and chest were easy in comparison, and soon were as smooth as silk.

He turned on the shower to lather himself again. The hot water felt good. Then he continued shaving his arms and legs and body, stopping every now and again to change to a new razor, and to lather on more soap. He began to sing as he saw himself getting smoother and smoother. He thought about Katrina. What she would think about the new Trevor.

He turned off the shower for the last time, and patted himself dry with a big towel. It was surprising how quickly he dried now that he was free of his hair. He splashed himself all over with the after-shave that he had bought in Boots. It stung, but he smelled wonderful. Then he carefully examined himself in the mirror to make sure that he hadn't missed any parts that he could reach. He knew he wasn't perfect, but he was pleased with what he saw.

His new jeans and the yellow Lacoste sweat-shirt, with its tell-tale alligator, the crocodile-skin cowboy boots, all looked great on him. He had never spent so much on clothes in his life. He looked at his clock, it had taken him over two hours to get ready. His heart was thudding as he walked out into the sunshine. Rosie was sitting on the grass outside her caravan with the reinforced concrete floor. She glanced at him as he walked past whistling, but she said nothing. 'Good,' he thought. 'She hasn't recognized me.' Two of the Dancing Dwarf Quads were sitting on the steps of their caravan drinking tea and they also ignored him. Trevor began to feel more confident about his chances.

He knocked on the door of Katrina's canary-yellow caravan. She opened it immediately and smiled at him.

'If you're looking for a job the manager's van is the big silver one at the end,' she said.

His heart leapt like a dolphin. She was wearing skin-tight black jeans and a low-cut pink blouse.

'I'm not after a job, Katrina. It's me, Trevor.'

'Trevor?'

'Yes. Trevor.'

'Well, hi, Trevor. What can I do for you?'

'I'd like to talk to you, Katrina. I've brought you these.' He handed her the Tesco's carrier bag containing the bottle of red wine and box of Roses chocolates.

She looked in the bag. 'Well, you're a cool customer I must say. I suppose you want me to tell your fortune.'

'I am your fortune, Katrina. And you are mine.'

She laughed loudly, and Trevor could see the pink inside of her mouth and the gold fillings in her back teeth.

'Oh, I could do with a fortune all right. I've told enough people that they're going to get one.'

'Can I come in, Katrina?'

'All right, but you can't stay long I've got work later on.'

She turned into the caravan, and he followed and closed the door behind him.

'Are you going to open the wine?' he asked.

'Might as well, seeing as you've brought it.' She poured out two glasses, and handed him one. 'So what are we drinking to?'

'Me and you.'

She smiled coyly. 'But I don't know you.'

'You soon will,' he said clinking his glass against hers.

She tossed her blue-black hair and flashed her eyes. 'Confident aren't you? I like the cowboy boots. Those must have set you back a bit. What do you do for a living then, Trevor?'

'You tell me, you're the fortune-teller,' he said offering her his hand.

She stared at his palm carefully. 'Interesting,' she said. 'You've had an interesting life.'

'Not really,' he said.

'You've been through some bad times.'

'That's true.'

'But your luck has changed. I see new horizons.'

'I hope so,' he said.

'Life is going to be a lot smoother for you.'

'That's certainly true,' he said, lifting her hand to his lips.

She smiled at him and he put his arms around her and kissed her. He looked into her eyes, they were as green as the sea and he felt as if he were drowning.

'Come away with me, Katrina,' he said, undoing the buttons of her blouse.

'Where to?' she asked, pulling his sweat-shirt up over his smooth chest.

'I've got some money, we could go anywhere Katrina,' he said unzipping her jeans.

'But Trevor. We hardly know each other,' she said leading him over to the bed.

Trevor quickly pulled off his crocodile-skin cowboy boots and his jeans and his pants and his socks.

'We do know each other, Katrina,' he said. 'I'm Trevor. Trevor that used to be the Wolf Man.'

'Wolf Man,' she said. 'Wolf Man, is it really you?' Her eyes travelled slowly over his body, and Trevor felt as if he was being bathed by a warm green sea. 'But Wolf Man, you're lovely.'

'Yes I am,' he said. 'I mean, I am Wolf Man, but I can't be Wolf Man any more. I'll lose my job now that I'm Trevor. Come away with me, Katrina.'

'Yes Trevor, I'll come with you,' she said.

'We'll leave in the morning,' he said. 'There's no point in hanging around here. We'll take a holiday first, go to Paris for a week.'

'Trevor,' she said. 'I don't want us to have secrets from

each other. So I'd better tell you now. I have another face.'

'I don't care how many faces you have, Katrina, I love you.'

'Yes, but I'm not really a fortune teller, Trevor. My other face is my fortune, and I think you should see my other face.'

'All right. But it won't make any difference. I love you, Katrina.'

She turned over onto her side, and lifted her heavy blue-black hair and parted it with her hands. He looked at the puckered blotched purple skin, the squashed blob of a nose, the angry raw slash of a mouth, and the mean misplaced lizard-like eyes staring back at him.

'Ugly, isn't it?' she said. 'I'm the Two Faced Woman that they come to stare at. I'm a freak.'

Trevor turned over to face the wall. He could feel her buttocks pressing against his, and her other mouth was nibbling at the back of his neck. Then her other face was travelling down his spine, pressing hard into the small of his back, reaching the only place that he hadn't been able to reach and where his hair grew thick.

'I love your fur, Wolf Man,' she said softly.

Deborah Chivers
Radio Baby

I'm pretty sure mother is going mad and now there's only me to notice. The new baby is snuffling in the small bedroom on the top floor, well away from us. I stand and listen to the baby from the bottom of the stairs. Mother says to turn on the radio whenever the baby starts to wail. She says the baby doesn't mean anything when it makes that sound, just turn up the radio, for God's sake. If she suspects I'm moving to the foot of the stairs to listen she calls me back and scolds me like I'm a six year old. I'm thinking perhaps I am; perhaps that's what I want to be. When I tell her the baby needs her, that he's hungry and cold, she gives me the look she used to when I was little and had been caught out in a lie. There is a perfectly good explanation, she says calmly, the child is tuning in ahead of me.

I caught a glimpse of the baby yesterday, when mother arrived home. I wasn't expecting her for another two days; she discharged herself ahead of time, phoning for a taxi. I had plans to clean the place up, maybe buy some flowers, at least get a meal ready before she got out. I was in the bath, my hair thick with shampoo when there was a knock on the front door. I stayed where I was; there are so many weird people calling these days, and I had no reason to expect anybody I knew. The knocking didn't stop so I got out of the bath and ran to the half-open landing window and peered through. There was mother leaning against the porch wall. I could see her thin blonde hair flying around her head and the pink seam of her scalp, like a plastic baby-doll's skull. Under her arm she was holding a bundle: on the ground a big blue plastic sack was sliding sideways. It was the sort of sack they give you for your belongings in hospital. As I stood there with the chilled shampoo-froth snaking down my shoulders, I was so tempted to leave the door unanswered. I knew when that door was opened any-thing could happen, so I stood for a while watching as mother shifted the bundle on to her hip and tipped forward to rest her forehead on the door.

In the kitchen I tried to hide the mountain of dirty dishes in the sink. I offered mother a cup of tea. First things first, she said, and manoeuvred the baby from her hip. It was a big, cumbersome boy with a rash across its upper lip. Mother unwound the bundle of blankets and dangled him like a little sack over her shoulder. I disliked the way its head lolled back and forth. Its neck seemed too weak for the job. Mother didn't look natural with the baby, and all the time she held it her face was contorted into what I took to be a smile. It comes over her when she hears the baby crying. After she had stood a while in the kitchen and looked at everything as if for the first time, she whirled around, saying she would put the baby in his place.

Mother has changed into her prettiest dress; marsh-mallow-pink with ruffles on the sleeves and around the hem. It's too wintry for this dress and her arms have erupted into goose bumps. I bring her a cardigan but she says no, it was so hot in there, she needs time to cool down. She hasn't washed since yesterday and she needs to. If I get up close I can smell souring milk and something else I can't identify. She refuses to answer my questions. I think she doesn't even hear them; she is listening for the baby, her body straining towards the hall, her mind's eye travelling up the long unlit passageway until it stops short at the closed cream door. The pink dress is girlish, too tight across her breasts. The mound of her belly pulls the front up so that I can see her bare knees. She is seeping milk into the bodice. The drying milk leaves the material stiff. I can tell her breasts are sore; she cradles them tenderly in her crossed arms, her face is flushed. I think she is developing a fever. All the time the radio plays. If she hears even the smallest scrap of commentary she starts forward, instantly animated. Oh no, she says, no words, no conversation, no stupid chat for God's sake, and fiddles with the dials to find music. When the room pulses with notes again she subsides.

Neither mother nor the baby is eating. I prepare her something I know she likes, but she looks at me with sly knowledge, as if she knows something about the food that I don't. The baby's cries have changed key, moved down an octave; he's tired of calling to her. When she fell into a brief, restless sleep earlier I crept up and stood outside the bedroom. I tried the handle but it was no good, mother's locked the door. I haven't seen the key. From inside the room I could hear a faint, thin, grizzling sound.

Now mother is rushing round the house closing the curtains. Something's coming, she says, something very important. I ask her what, what, but she doesn't answer me. As she walks away I see that smudges of blood are blooming in the seated pink fabric at the back of her dress, some fresh, some older and darker. Over her shoulder she says we could go out, if it wasn't for the radio. I follow close behind. And the baby, I say, we mustn't leave the baby. She turns slowly to face me. Mmmm, yes, the radio-baby, she says, and nods, narrowing her eyes and tapping the side of her nose with an index finger. She looks like the wicked witch in an amateur pantomime. I feel like shouting 'O yes you do.' Throughout the day the door has been knocked on several times. She indicates no, I'm not to answer, and blocks my way with her body.

It's late in the evening now, and mother has been perched for hours like some crazy bird on the arm of a chair in the lounge. Sit there, she coaxes me, pointing vaguely. The baby is silent. The radio is singing in the kitchen. Here in the lounge the hi-fi radio is on. Messages are about to come through, she tells me. We must listen for instructions, make sure we're tuned in. I ask will there be anything on the radio to tell us what to do about the baby. She slides down from the arm of the chair and reclines crookedly on the seat like a rag-doll, her legs apart. Her face gleams dully in the small light from the hi-fi. Keep still, she shouts, I'm about to take a message, find a pen and some paper. I'm counting, she says in a playful, childish tone. If I get to ten and you're not back, I'll come and find you, then the fun'll begin.

Mother has counted to eight by the time I get back to the lounge. I sit opposite her and see she has been counting on her fingers. This way I don't make silly mistakes, she says, holding both hands up. We sit and listen to the radio. Mother starts to doodle on the paper, every now and then stopping to listen. I'm drawing the child in the room upstairs, she says, and holds up the page. She has drawn a naked baby lying in some grass. From the neck down it appears normal, but where its head should be there is a radio. Notes float up from the radio's mouth. Then I see that instead of an umbilical cord the baby has an electric flex coming out of its navel. The flex floats up towards the top of the page and ends in an unconnected plug. I ask her what does it mean. It's the radio-baby she says patiently, as if I'm incredibly stupid. We sit on in the room. Mother adjusts the radio's controls, patting and stroking it at intervals. Soon I'll know what to do, she says, I've only got to wait, the message will come through eventually. I try to keep watch, but I feel myself falling, swooning into sleep. Through my dreams the radio plays, and far, far off, in amongst the notes, a baby cries, like a little interlude, and then is abruptly quiet. I wake up. The curtains are open and the radio is silent. There is an atmosphere of waiting that seems to tremble off the pale walls of the house. I hear mother treading heavily down the stairs. She pushes the lounge door open and walks towards me. I see a fresh, dark smudge on her cheek. There, she says, giving me the bedroom door-key and dusting her hands, I've turned off that radio for good.

Lewis Davies
Mr Roopratna's Chocolate

Mr Roopratna brushed leaves in the Palm Garden. He must have been working when I arrived to take the bungalow. Three rooms, two I didn't need and a kitchen. I checked the locks on the windows, the water running from the shower. It dribbled out, warm and salty.

'It is better in the evening,' DeSilva cut a wide white smile. 'Now it's the dry months, low pressure in the afternoon.'

It was cheap; the village was sliding into the off season and the stream of German tourists had also dropped to a trickle as the monsoon gathered patiently out in the ocean.

'There's a good gardener, very good.' He nodded to make sure I understood.

Mr. Roopratna was waiting in the darkness of the verandah when I returned from a bar at the beach. The sun had dipped quickly under the sea, flooding the jungle in a deep whispering night of bats and cicadas high in the trees. He bowed reverently and pointed to the door. His lips opened quickly enunciating a request in a burst of unfamiliar words.

I pointed towards the bungalow and he nodded in agreement, his eyes gleaming when I switched on a light which flickered uneasily in bursts of low current. Brown skin was stretched taut across a thin face, shining where hair thinned to wisps of grey on his scalp. His chest was bare and faded grey trousers rose from his calves to be secured at his waist with a black leather belt.

'You're the gardener.'

He nodded vigorously.

I offered my hand which he shook very shyly; then stood still, only returning my smile.

'Can I help you?'

He pointed at the light switch and then further into the bungalow where the corridor twisted back to the bedrooms.

'Rooms yes, light?'

He nodded again and pointed. Then moved a few steps into the wide, open kitchen beckoning me to follow him. His feet, bare and calloused, echoed faintly in the hollow stillness of the bungalow, barely glancing the ochre tiles on the floor.

At the back of the bungalow where the bathroom edged into the jungle he pointed to a door I had not seen when I had first been shown the rooms. It was locked from the outside.

Mr Roopratna flicked a light switch on the wall, quickly bowed and retreated from the entrance.

I looked through one of the cracks in the planed wooden door to the room beyond. A sink, a few tattered shelves and a palm mat on the floor. I pulled away sharply as Mr Roopratna shuffled in from his own side entrance.

I retreated back to my own room. I had not been expecting to share the bungalow. I thought about the stranger in the next room as the fan stirred listlessly below the ceiling, brushing the brittle mesh of the mosquito net against my skin.

The first weeks drifted easily. I stretched out wide canvasses under the verandah and painted the hanging fronds of palm trees and quick lithe motions of children as they climbed down from the village on the hill to collect water from the deep clear well in the garden.

I liked to imagine I was working hard, rising at seven to catch the thick early light which dripped in through the trees from the East. But Mr Roopratna was always working earlier, brushing leaves from the weeping trees into tidy piles. Moving slowly, he cornered each one with the constant trush, trush of his brushing, corralling them into corners. The leaves played with him, teasing his time, and by the following morning a new flock would have settled and he would resume his journey around the wide, tree-filled garden.

In the afternoons I read, the heavy heat of a thickening monsoon congealing the life of the garden until even the Roller singing from the high branches of a jackfruit tree fell silent.

Mr Roopratna would retreat to the shade of the coconut palms and deliberately sharpen the blade of a scythe or just sit, eyes half-closed, rocking gently.

He began speaking to me on the third morning when I practiced my newly learned words of Sinhalese, strange sounds that stuttered uncomfortably across my tongue. He understood them in a broad, surprised smile and replied in a long monologue that left me smiling for minutes while he leaned on his brush talking freely and pointing.

I tried to paint his movements, but he had a grace that frustrated before finally defeating my clumsy efforts. His arms and legs seemed to move without strain through the turgid heat, while my own smudged their form upon a succession of abandoned canvasses.

He came to see a third attempt when he realised I was

watching his progress. His face drew to a grin which he stifled to a serious nod.

In the evenings he began to sit in the light of the verandah talking quietly to himself, while I continued with the books I used to shorten the night. He wouldn't drink the beer I offered him but liked the expensive chocolate I bought from the Oriental Hotel, treating each square as the rarest of luxuries.

Geckos, pale to the walls, watched us as I plotted progress.

But the canvasses were not shaping as I wanted them. The oil was drying too fast and I couldn't mix the deep greens that merged with the forest.

At the end of the first month DeSilva arrived by rickshaw to collect his rent. He was a large, genial man whose expansive gestures emphasised his natural generosity.

'Are you sure you can afford to pay? Pay me next week, perhaps you have more money then?' He accepted a glass of arrack and relaxed into one of his own rattan chairs.

'Perhaps you take the house for six months? No?'

I shook my head.

'I think you like it here, you work well, you're a painter yes?'

I nodded my agreement despite my stubborn canvasses.

We drank further from the arrack. It was a thin golden alcohol that climbed into my head quickly.

'The gardener, he speaks to me in the mornings.'

DeSilva laughed easily.

'He is a good man, you don't worry about him.'

'No, not worried, just can't understand what he says. He speaks no English.'

'He talks about his sons, they are in the Navy at Trinco.'

'His sons?'

'Yes and about sweeping the leaves at Buckingham

Palace. He thinks he sweeps leaves for the Queen of England.' He waved his arms to indicate his garden. 'She would like it here I think.'

Another week meandered. Mr Roopratna corralled more leaves and continued to talk to me in the mornings. I learned the words for sons out of my phrase book and his smile, never far below the surface broadened with a deep pride. He brought a smudged black and white photograph from his room of two dark boys spruced clean in uniform at a parade.

'Trinco,' He pointed east, Matara side.

'Are you from Trinco?'

He nodded in agreement, but DeSilva claimed he was from a village twenty miles along the South coast, Badulla side. Trinco was two hundred miles away on the East.

He held the photograph proudly as he pointed to the sailors, then to his own chest.

'Fine sons.' My language extended to little more. Mr Roopratna put the photograph away.

The following week DeSilva arrived with a bag full of house paints and a little girl he introduced as his daughter. The girl was shy and twisted around behind her father's legs to hide from the white stranger.

'For you, yes?' He pointed at the paints, opening the bag to reveal bright reds, yellows and greens in litre tins.

'House paints?'

'Yes, yes.' He guided me enthusiastically into the bungalow. A wide white wall dominated the room. 'A painting here.'

I retreated from the wall.

'Er, I paint, er people, trees.'

'Yes, here. The big hotels in Hikkaduwa, they all have wall paintings, you paint here?' The wall pushed out; white.

'Trees and people.'

His daughter whispered to him in Sinhalese and he swung her up into his arms.

'She says she would like elephants in it, like at Kandy.'

He refused the arrack, looking down to his daughter for explanation, but stayed to discuss his plans for the Palm Garden. There was room for another bungalow in the corner where he had planted a string of stubborn banana plants that had refused to flourish as he had expected.

'I think the soil poor there, too much salt.'

The village was twisting itself further to the requirements of wealthy Germans and Swiss escaping the European winter with a crop of new hotels rising slowly just beyond the fringe of the lagoon.

'This year was good but next year who knows? I build this and no-one comes. I think the troubles will start again, then everything quiet.'

'You think the peace will break?'

'We are waiting now, they do not talk anymore, and when they do it is just words.'

He looked around for the young girl.

'Bandi?'

She came running from the garden clutching a crimson flower Mr Roopratna had given her.

I enjoyed painting the mural. It was the first thing that had come easily for five months. I mixed the green darker, colouring a thick luxuriant jungle with a river plunging into a waterfall before bursting out onto a plain filled with elephants. Monkeys hung from the trees, cheerful and human. It was a long way from my canvasses of vague brushed expressionism.

Mr Roopratna watched me for longer now as I daubed the white wall into colour. Gasps of admiration had greeted my big brown elephants and he spoke the word *Wandura* when the monkeys appeared, then pointed out to the jack-fruit tree where a troop sometimes settled in the late evening to feast.

The painting was a success. Mr Roopratna called a band of children who had come down to drag water from the well into the doorway to view the scene. They whispered to themselves, pointing to the wall before edging back with faint apologies when I invited them closer.

He also asked to borrow my radio, which I used to remind me of the world beyond. Things I could remember about the news and strange, unusual reports from Singapore and Dacca as private tragedies became public entertainment.

He listened to it in the afternoon, earnestly trying to find a frequency that would talk to him, a blur of light, far away language carrying over from beneath the palms.

'It is very good.'
DeSilva was delighted with the mural. He edged up closer, a critic dissecting the work.
'Many colours.'
Its fame spread quickly and within a week I had three commissions from the village on the hill. Another forest scene, Buddha and a leopard for the school. I was paid with food; coconuts, boiled jack and a bag full of freshly dried cashews.

Mr Roopratna proudly led me down to the Hotel Ocean for a fourth. He talked volubly to a young waiter who had joined him for the performance.

I was enjoying the work and gave up my canvasses completely, preferring to fish from the headland in the early morning. Mullet drifted through the clear water, teasing me with their ignorance of my hook, while fishermen in short wooden catamarans waved as they skirted the shallows.

I take a week to travel North into the hill country. Paddybirds fly low over the water scattering reflections that flap through the rippled surface of narrow lakes fringing the coast road.

Further north a crowded bus twists through a jungle thick with people. At each town the bus is surrounded by children selling peanuts and chewing gum. Their brown faces smile expectantly at my white, inspired by the novelty and hope of an easy sale.

A man selling shoes and speaking fluent English shares my seat as far as Wellawaya. He talks briefly of the war. 'It is bad. They ask too much. One half of the country. It is too much. We will have to defeat them.'

His shoes are shiny patent reds and black in imitation leather.

'I have a friend in Germany. He writes to me every year. Good friend.'

He picks out a colour polaroid of a big German with a huge, smiling moustache from his wallet.

'Business partner. One day I go to Germany. Very good country. No troubles there.'

At Ela I wait out a few days, drinking tea looking down over the stubby bushes which pattern the hills to the plains far below. The air is fresher than the thick shimmering heat of the plains. In the evening I wait for the blink of a lighthouse a hundred miles away on the coast at Matara, reminding me of the Palm Garden. The afternoons drift. I spend a few hours hitching down to a waterfall on the road a thousand feet below. A quick swim in the plunge pool, then a slow sweet journey back up in the cab of a lorry, two men delivering sugar into the hill country from South of Wellawaya. Strong sweet smells of the newly refined sugar stay with me in memory.

I write a string of postcards. To Mr Roopratna an elephant adorned for the Pahera at Kandy. I struggle with a strange script and easy phrases, hoping he will understand.

When I return to the Palm Garden I ask about the card, but he only shakes his head sadly as if feeling my disappointment.

Towards the middle of April the monsoon lost patience with the season and made its first afternoon raids along the coast, as if some marauding pirate intent on riches. The rain fell heavy and straight out of a jungle black sky. More leaves fell into the Palm Garden. Mr Roopratna was slower in their retrieval and spent more time listening to the radio in the early evenings. I filled the spaces with long, fat meaningless books and tried to ignore a chorus of frogs that sang enthusiastically, welcoming the rain.

Celebrations to usher the start of the New Year were beginning in the village, marked by a procession of pilgrims and a bicycle race. Fireworks escaped early from their dry calm, scattering sparks and thunderclaps throughout the houses beneath the trees.

Mr Roopratna appeared to wither as the celebrations gained momentum, and a day before the official New Year he was waiting for me on the verandah with a crumpled newspaper. He pointed to the script, which I couldn't understand, but there was a blurred photograph tacked onto the front page. It looked like a ship lying forlorn on its side in shallow water, its hull and purpose holed at the waterline; dark scars of a fierce fire marked the metal.

'Trinco?'

He nodded sadly.

'Your sons?'

His head dropped as he mumbled to himself before retreating to the rear of the bungalow.

The world service gave the barest of details. A suicide

attack on a gunship at Trincomalee. The Tigers had claimed responsibility. There were seventeen dead. Another quick, brutal tragedy was carried briefly before they moved onto another, the execution of a housemaid in Singapore.

The morning of the New Year I climbed the hill to the village in the jungle. I was still being paid for a mural in kindness and invites. I clutched a box of biscuits as a gift for the family. The meal arrived in a burst of smiles and small dishes of brinjal and fish curry. I settled back to eat and the family settled back to watch me.

They kept pointing to my mural on the wall. A bright easy leopard which snarled out at the children who pretended to be frightened when they played hide and seek with their hands. A couple of neighbours shuffled in to see the visitor eating, armed with shy requests for work.

When I climbed back down to the Palm Garden to the final crescendo of daylight fireworks DeSilva was waiting with a rickshaw, another daughter and an invite.

'You will come for the feast.'

'Now?'

'Yes, big feast this afternoon.'

The rickshaw moved quickly on the strangely empty roads. People had retreated home for the holiday. DeSilva's daughter talked excitedly to her father.

'She's asks about the gardener. She likes him.'

'His sons?'

'Yes, his sons. They came to collect him this morning.'

'I thought they were in Trinco? The bombing?'

'No no, they're on leave. They came to take him back to his wife for the New Year.'

'His wife?'

The flow of words accelerated beyond the rickshaw as

my fixed imagination re-focused hazily.

'Yes he has a wife and daughters, Badulla side. He goes to visit them every two months or so.'

The girl at his side added another question, which he answered but didn't translate.

A week passes after the New Year. I begin again on my canvasses, but the garden seems very quiet without Mr Roopratna. The visiting monkeys are miserable and silent, subdued by the rain and distrusting of the slippery branches, now such treacherous friends. The monsoon has filled the wells higher in the village and even the children stay away. Only the Roller remains a constant, colouring the mornings.

I buy pineapples from the village and drink arrack in the nights while I plan a flight back, listening to the reports of an escalating war in the North.

I had bought a big bar of chocolate for Mr Roopratna, which waited for him in the fridge.

When DeSilva arrived for his final month's rent I ask him to make sure the old man receives the gift.

DeSilva smiles sadly.

'I'm sorry, I can't. He died a week ago.'

'Died?'

'Hospital. They took him in, not come out.'

'What of?'

DeSilva shrugged his shoulders.

'You come back next year?'

Joyce Herbert
The Sadness of Doctor Mendoza

The swing doors of Fernando's restaurant flapped and squeaked when the waiters slid in and out: slices of light came through with the voices of diners and were lost in the dark. The bravest people took their coffee outside: it wasn't really warm enough yet, but something drew them there although the tables were still damp with the day's rain. There was a smell of dried seaweed and fish from the market round the corner, also the smell of the sea straight off the breakers. Doctor Mendoza, pausing to breathe it as he came out, frowned when Mrs Ingram called to him.

'Bonsoir, Monsieur le Médecin. Come and have a coffee. Don't rush off like that. Come on.'

He inclined his head and joined her, bowing as he reached her table. He found conversation with his fellow-diners at Fernando's a tedious business, since foreigners always irritated him, particularly in early spring when he felt melancholy. Mrs Ingram had found out that he spoke French, and practised hers on him whenever she could, promising to take him in hand in the summer and teach him English.

She was sitting bolt upright in her blue trews and sailor's

jersey, as if she was on a horse. Her long leathery face, nearly as brown as his own: the sunburn of an English blonde. Each day she cooked herself on the beach, lying on her towel in her bikini and turning herself to numbers as she used to so long ago at Nice and Bandol and Menton: her short grey hair was newly set: her bony face could still be charming with its quirky smile, but it was wary.

She took out her cigarettes as soon as the doctor sat down, and he was ready with his lighter, knowing she would take his wrist out of long habit, which she did, but delicately, as if she was afraid.

'You must have a brandy, Madame,' he said, extending the tip of a forefinger to the small boy who waited in the shadows for the slightest hint of their needs. The child approached gravely and stood a little way off, his shoulders stooping in deference, his eyes beating off sleep and hardly functioning. The doctor ordered the drinks without looking at him, but Mrs Ingram smiled at him and sighed noisily.

'Poor little man, he can't be more than twelve. I can never get used to seeing such babies kept up until midnight and working so hard. What time do they have to play like other children? I never see them paddling on the beach.'

The doctor narrowed his eyes, paddling on the beach, what a twittering fool the woman was.

'They are the children of the poor. They are lucky to find work in a restaurant. These days they are in heaven. Their wages are very good.'

'But you're a doctor. Don't you think they're too young?'

'That's their parents' affair.' He tapped his mouth gently with his cigar. 'They are very strong. Our peasants are the strongest in the world, it is well known.'

'But you've lived in France. They don't work children of that age in France.' The brandy was making her argumentative. She was still managing to sound flirtatious, but he sensed the kind of patronage he disliked most.

'In France? They had a revolution in France, didn't they? Their ways are not our ways. You had a revolution, too, didn't you murder your king long before the French did? Revolutions are bad, they lead to attitudes we don't share in Portugal, although we have hotheads here, as there are everywhere. The poor don't want money, they need guidance always, you understand. They are stupid.'

Mrs Ingram was losing interest, but she stirred herself and tapped him on the arm.

'Naughty Portuguese! You treat women abominably, too. Not even allowed to vote.'

'Why should they want to do such a thing? A woman shouldn't he concerned with politics. To be agreeable to a man, that's what matters, isn't it?' He grinned scornfully.

Mrs Ingram showed her long yellow teeth in return. She shrugged, and smoked and pushed at her sunbleached hair that was so overtinted it looked like seaweed. What's the use, she seemed to say, these Portuguese are all the same. When the boy brought her brandy she smiled at him and gave him all the escudos from the bottom of her handbag. Doctor Mendoza didn't smile.

'You are not helping him by doing that,' he said.

'I don't care. I like children.'

His huge jowl relaxed slightly. 'Have you any of your own?'

'Three. And four grandchildren.'

A kind of concern moved behind his dull black eyes like the gleam within coal, they were so black and bottomless they drowned his thoughts with ease.

'Do you see them often? Will you see them soon?' He put the fingertips of one hand gently on those of the other and nodded slightly, his method when questioning patients. She looked away.

'Well, perhaps not soon. They write, of course, send photographs of the children, and at Christmas everyone writes. Times like that. They have their own lives to live, their friends and all the rest of it.'

He was appalled. 'But they must worry about you, living so far away from home, and on your own?'

'Not on your life. I can look after myself, anyway. Everyone has to, nowadays. Of course if I were ill I daresay there'd be some action, great fuss... but we understand each other. They know me of old. Living in England is impossible with all the taxation, I could never cope with it. All the things one cherished have gone, you know. It isn't England any more. No manners, impossible to get servants unless you pay the earth, and then they're hopeless. Everything's gone wrong there, and if you had investments before the war it's impossible to live as you would wish to. I have to look after myself in this world, and the way the currency is being restricted Portugal will be getting too expensive for me, and I'm terribly afraid I'll have to go to Spain, and I prefer it here. I like the people, they're so kind, and I don't like Spaniards.'

The doctor also disliked Spaniards but he admired them too. They made him feel inferior. But he said nothing. She was looking about her, so he waved his forefinger again.

'Another brandy.'

'Oh, dear. I shouldn't really. It's my turn. No, really you mustn't. Very well, you naughty man, but my treat next time.'

The boy stood near them, his napkin over his patient arm. She smiled vaguely at him and watched him move away.

'Have you any children, Doctor?' She folded her hands and rested her long chin on them; she thought he was still good-looking with his insatiable eyes in a face of carved mahogany, his white hair en brosse. She liked his cream linen suit, his huge Panama hat which he could doff with such an air. She stared into his eyes.

'I have a son,' he said at last. 'He's a doctor also, he lives in Lisbon.'

'How nice. Married?'

'Yes, with four children. Two sons and two daughters.'

'Really. Of course I knew you were a widower. We have something in common, Doctor.' She looked at her glass and sighed.

'My wife died when my son was born. I live alone, which is why I eat at Fernando's quite often. They're good cooks and they know how I like my food prepared.'

'Aren't you lonely though? You must be, sometimes....' She put her head on one side and showed the whites of her eyes. Thinking how he hated elderly coquettes, he sighed.

'Alas, yes. But I have my friends and my books, I have my practice and I know everyone here and they know me. My family have lived here for many generations.' He spoke slowly and patiently as though to a child. She is casting her net, he thought.

'You've been alone a long time, poor man.' She was arranging her bony legs more comfortably, nestling in her chair. There was a long silence. The fountain in the square trickled sharply into it. They were the last patrons and in the shadows the boy waited.

The doctor sighed again. The underlying warmth in the air, the tug of the great sun in it preparing to attack, the brandy, began to dislodge ancient sorrows as they always did. He felt pleasantly melancholy, wished there was someone singing Fado while the breakers hammered the boiling sand. He leaned forward and looked intense.

'She died many years ago, my dear wife, but I hoped to remarry one day and I met a most beautiful girl. She was like an angel.'

Mrs Ingram sat erect and drank some more brandy.

'But how fascinating. Tell me all about it,' she said, stretching her lips back from her long teeth and opening

70

her eyes wide.

'There isn't much to tell,' mournfully, 'and it is very sad.'

'Where did you meet her? Did she live here?'

'She was Spanish. I met her when I was working in Madrid. I shall never forget her. I loved her so much.'

'Then why ever didn't you marry her?' Mrs Ingram was feeling the brandy like a little warm tongue on her body.

'We were going to be engaged. She came from a very old Castilian family, very distinguished. You know what Spanish aristocrats are like. Very proud. It was a good match, they had so much land.....'

'Then what went wrong?' Mrs Ingram's cigarette was nearly burning her fingers.

'My mother wasn't willing for me to marry again.' His eyes searched the darkness of the square. She hit her mouth with her palm and gasped.

'Your mother? Good God, how old were you?'

'Thirty-six. That's how it is in Portugal. Always the mother. You don't understand. No good arguing. The mother always decides.'

'Then how old was your girlfriend?'

'Eighteen. A pearl. A star. My Dolores.'

'You poor thing, you. What a ghastly thing. But really, you know, you should have gone straight ahead and done what you wanted to do. Your mother would have come round in the end.' She finished her brandy and looked about. The boy sidled nearer.

'Two more brandies, dear. Yes, I insist, my treat. Here you are, little boy. Now, do go on, tell me what happened. Your fiancée must have been heartbroken, I know I would have been.'

'Of course. It was a disgrace for a Spanish girl of that class to be jilted. She was sent to a convent at once. An enclosed Order, too. Carmelites, very strict. She's still there of course. Will always be there.'

71

'My God, how barbarous.' Mrs Ingram took up her glass, her eyes glistening. He didn't much like the word barbarous.

'It was the correct thing for a girl from such a family. She would have been disgraced. I was desolate. Ever since I have been desolate.'

'Poor you. Poor Doctor Mendoza.'

'I am quite alone. I am sixty years old. She is forty-two, now.'

'Do you write to each other?' She wanted a romantic ending, pen friends at least.

'Write? Of course not. It would not be correct. Besides, she has brothers. They'd soon be after my blood. They would kill me. I hear of her sometimes, a few words, through a mutual friend.'

She shook her head and though how savage it all sounded. Presently he groped for his umbrella.

'I think I will go home now. Shall I escort you to your flat?'

She started. 'No, thanks, really. It would be so out of your way.'

'But I insist. Come along, we'll go together.' He helped her up with his courtesy that had kept a little gallantry in it, wiping his lips with a slight flourish of his silk handkerchief, just patting them lightly, bowing and standing back.

'Madame,' he said, offering his arm.

'I shall never forget what you told me. So sad,' as they walked past the fish market and along the sea front.

'That is life. We all have our own tragedies.'

'Poor Doctor Mendoza,' she said, and stopped suddenly. 'No need to come any further. You carry on. I'll nip up that little hill and I'll be home in a jiffy.' She turned away as she spoke.

'But are you sure you'll be all right?' His hand climbed towards his Panama.

'Of course. See you tomorrow. Boa noite.' She ran off, waving vigorously. The hill slowed her pace but still she ran, head down, her white handbag banging against her legs. She thought what a dear he was and so good-looking in a sombre sort of way. How black his hair must have been: it still seemed to struggle under that bleached-looking white, the drowned night of his passions seething still. His eyes were so black they looked blind.

She shivered, for the wind off the sea was ice-cold. At the top of the hill she stopped and listened. Doctor Mendoza also stopped and listened. He stepped back into an alleyway, then peeped out carefully and saw what he expected to see. Mrs Ingram, formerly of Esher, sure of herself now that she couldn't hear his footsteps, was running back toward the square, her thin legs stabbing the cobblestones, her handbag flapping up and down.

He knew where she was going and laughed silently. Johnny's Bar would be full of expatriates, and there'd be the usual gigolos with guitars. She would drink herself silly, head lolling and arms flailing, until one of the men took her home.

He was always surprised at the way these people lived. He was sure their countries must be on the verge of collapse, and often said so to his friends. He walked on toward his Villa Rosa. The wind plucked at his linen suit, but it didn't matter; soon the flowers would be blazing everywhere. He remembered the waitress at Fernando's and smiled sideways, she had let him pick at her breasts when he passed her on his way to the dining-room. She had a thick, broad body and hair as coarse as a horse's tail: just the sort of girl he liked. The moon slid behind a cloud, and appeared again. He stood looking at it, his hand on the gate of his villa. The remnants of his melancholy returned and gathered quietly, but not strongly enough to hurt too much. He sighed gently.

'How very sad I feel,' he thought, and went inside slowly, swinging his umbrella in a jaunty way.

Rae Howells
A Bleak Future without Thought-Paper

Do you know what I did today? I was distracted from my writing by an unknown presence in the house. Of course, I was compelled to explore. In the bedroom, I opened up my wardrobe and there I found a whirling, spewing, swirl of light, and I dipped my head into it to see what would happen. It turned out, strangely enough, to be exactly what I expected: a gateway, a tunnel, a bridge to the future.

The future took me by surprise at first. It splashed me in the face like a pan of cold water. I flinched, everything swayed, and then I was there, in it. It had not been seamless, but apparently, the future had swallowed me, and made me a part of itself. I was in the body of someone old, and the longer I stayed there, the more confused my thoughts became.

I am washing. My stomach is big and wrinkled and sort of tight. Someone is calling me. My voice is weak, and warbles its reply. Everywhere sags and is alien to me, and yet strange because I am inside the skin, and I feel each stroke of my hands upon it. Everything is slightly duller; something I may not have noticed with the gradual passage of time, yet which leaps out at me as it is presented in such contrast to my young life. I finish washing, but then I find that it is hard to know whether I washed myself at all: I can't remember; I do it again. It is mundane, and my mind wanders. I look around, and I am shocked to find that the walls are the walls of my own house, though they have aged considerably, and the colour is different.

On the ceiling, there are circles formed in the paint. Funny how I never noticed them before, not consciously.

Why am I looking at the ceiling? Look! – there are circles, yes, definite circular patterns in the yellow paint. How strange. I am washing. I rinse. I get up, and find a towel on the radiator. It is warm and comforting, and I am chewing its corner.

A voice. The door opens, I gaze at it vacantly.

'All washed, dear? All clean? Ray?' Me – he means me. Ah, my sweetheart called me that, long, long ago. He called me Ray. He looks like Howard sometimes, when this old man smiles, I can see a shadow of Howard there behind his eyes, and hiding in the corners of his mouth. I nod. There – Howard, in his smile.

'Howard?'

'Yes dear, it's Howard. Let's get you dressed.'

I wander dreamily with him, as he shepherds me into a small room at the back of the house. My face lights up. My photographs are here – I see them – they're in a big shoe box. I go straight to them. I feel like a small girl again, with liberty to go where I please. He gives me freedom to look, while he prattles on about my long blue skirt and my navy cardigan. He says he remembers me as a young girl, of eighteen or so. How thin I was, how proud he was. There is a photograph here. Me in my twenties, with thin legs and dark eyes. Hmm. I'm almost her again today.

I look up and I'm dressed. He is talking. He looks at me and smiles to find me watching. He looks like Howard – his eyes, they could almost be his, a little more lined, a little more watery, but Howard's.

'I thought we'd go to the park today,' he is saying. 'That would be nice wouldn't it? We can feed the ducks, or have an ice-cream.'

'Ice-cream,' I echo. 'Can we go to Joe's, or Verdi's, like we used to? Can we have hot chocolate and teacakes by the sea?'

'We'll see, dearest. It might be nicer to have ice-cream in the park, at that new coffee bar. We had it last week, didn't we? You said it was the nicest ice-cream you'd ever tasted.'

'Don't be ridiculous! You must be confusing it with something else. I certainly wasn't at the park last week.' My memory is so dark, like a fog, locking away the things I should remember.

When I've eaten my boiled egg, and changed my cardigan because of the yellow dribble on its front, we put on our coats, and he takes my arm, and we walk out of the house, and down the garden, overgrown with yellowing, choked brambles. It is an autumn day, sunny but cold. I remember one like it; oh yes, the smell is almost the same. I breathe it in, deep. Straight off the sea.

'It reminds me of Christmas,' I say.

'It's getting colder,' he replies.

I am thrown back to a recollection from many years ago. The sea, crashing all around, and the freezing wind whipping our voices around us as we cling together in the strange orange light of the streetlamps, and the clouds in the yellow pallor of the moon as they scud like things surreal and possessed across the sky. Freezing and frightening, and humbling, and rawly beautiful.

Today is stiller, and seems to have no significance.

I think I wrote about it once. As a young woman these things fascinated me. Weren't those days wonderful, weren't they?

He is pulling a plastic bag out of his pocket, saying 'I know how much you love to feed the ducks.' Howard used to throw bread at the ducks, enticing them over with scraps, and then bombing them with bread-bullets when they came close enough. Howard had always done silly, stupid things, just for the sake of fun.

Oh God. A cruel flash. I am spliced by a stab of insight that slips through me and takes my breath. It seems so awfully *sad* to be stuck here inside myself, me, with the loss of my own tools; wit, reason, intelligence, memory. Who plays with us? It cannot be mere chance for I could have overcome blindness, but how can I overcome when I have no faculties? If it were chance, I should not have suffered at the hands of some being's clever torture.

My reality is only different from yours. One day I woke up and I was somewhere else, had been displaced, and as the gap widened the bridge between all your realities and mine, instead of stretching, snapped. I float. Now thinking is a rainbow curl of oily petrol, tumbling through the rapids and lost, so inevitably, drowned out and crushed by the roar of the waterfall.

If I had some paper... I could dip it into the pool of my head and marble it with my thoughts. Thought-paper. How else will my thoughts ever get out? I want to – what?

'Do you want some more bread?' He puts his arm around me. 'You almost looked like the old Ray then,' he says quietly, half to me, half to himself. But I turn away, because I don't quite know who he is. I take the bread with a weak smile, and throw it half-heartedly at the ducks, who eat it indiscriminately.

In my head I can almost see a pure thought as it runs ahead of me through the fog, like a shade, mingling with the mists before it takes shape, and then fades before I can make it out. I despair – briefly – I don't think anything ever lasts. The fog, the vagueness, thickens. He thrusts an ice-cream at me. I eat it, and watch his eyes. I think I must love this man. He seems so familiar, as if he is always there, but I'm not so sure quite who he is.

Maybe I knew him once. (Maybe he knew me once.)

I eat my ice-cream, quite content. Its cold dribbles are sharp on my hand, sharper than they once were – my very bones seem chilled these days. Always cold, always exposed. I shiver. He sees me (he's been watching me, with the eagle eye of a toddler's mother), and he puts my scarf around my neck more thoroughly. I notice the details, perhaps they give me a framework, something to grab hold of in the brief moment before they fade like so much else.

I realise I must have been rambling, because he's talking again, replying to something I must have said. I try to work it out....

A small child is dangerously close to the water's edge, but his mother is there – the ducks fight with the crows for scraps of food nearby – an elderly couple with a dog walk slowly by, stopping at the ancient, disused drinking fountain, and try in vain to move the pump handle, like so many others before them. Hmm?

'Ray? Let's go, love, let's go. You're tired.'

A flash of anger at being told how I feel. I am about to snap, but.

We are at home again. I cease to wonder how these small miracles happen. Where does the mundane go? It is teatime, apparently. Lunch has been and gone, I am told we had sardine sandwiches. I have also been to sleep, and now I have to take my tablets, and eat again. It might seem like an endless cycle if I could remember any of it. Just face the now, Ray, just try to face the moment.

Chips and beans. Howard's favourite! His, too, no doubt: A meal with no nutritional value, just plain indulgence.

'You know my Howard loved chips and beans. They

were his favourite. I cooked them every Saturday teatime for years and years, just to give him a treat. Of course, we'd eat vegetables the rest of the time, but he looked forward to Saturdays just for his treat. He loved me, you know. We were married for, well, years and years. I wonder whatever happened to him. He was my special boy, you know. We had Rhia and Tom. Tom Bombadil, Howard called him, and in the end he nagged Howard so much, that he ended up having *The Lord of the Rings* read to him, bit by bit, every bedtime. We had so much fun, so much love, all the good times together. I wonder where they all can be now. They've all left me.'

I look up to see him wiping a tear from his cheek.

'I'm Howard,' he says. '*I'm* Howard.'

A flash! – 'Yes dear, you're my Howard, aren't you. I see him in your smile. Come here and hold me. We love each other, don't we, we're happy, aren't we?'

'Of course, my love, we are happy, and I love you as much as I ever did.'

But bliss is shortlived, and no sooner has he left the room to bring me my plate and my cup of tea, than he seems like a stranger again.

I thank him with appropriate politeness. He reminds me to take my pills when my tea has cooled down enough; he watches to make sure as if I am a child.

'You know I love you Ray, don't you?'

'Oh yes.'

He is writing.

'We had such a lovely day today, didn't we? Do you remember what we did?'

I gave him a troubled look; I am running through the dark, and all around me curling shapes pretend to be what they are not.

'We went to the park like we always used to. And this afternoon, you fell asleep in my arms while I stroked your

80

hair, like I always did when we were young, do you remember?'

'Howard?'

'Ray – I love you so much, Ray, and I want you to understand that what I do is for us both. It's the best way. What would you do without me? It's for the best. Now eat your tea. I just wanted you to know, that's all.'

I eat. Perhaps something important is happening. I struggle, but the shade eludes me.

He finishes; we both do. He clears the plates and washes them. Everything is tidy.

'Have you taken your tablet? I don't think you have,' he says. He hands me some water, and a pill, and I see another one on the table, and I take mine, and he takes his, and he lies down on the sofa next to me and holds me close and strokes my hair, and tells me he loves so much, so much, and the fog swirls, deeper and deeper and faster and faster. We drift away together

right, right away.

The present returns like a pan of cold water splashed in my face.

That's what I did today.

Jo Hughes
Forbidden Fruits

The Steadman women had elegance. Even from an early age, the two daughters seemed to possess some other worldly grace that Mari could only dream of.

The daughters had long blonde straight hair that always hung sleekly and cleanly down their backs, and they walked gracefully, like models on a cat walk, even though one of them was only nine and the other eleven. They had voices that seemed to be honey sweet and you never heard them curse or shriek. Not even if a wasp suddenly flew into their faces or they stepped barefoot into something nasty hidden in the long grass.

They got their good looks from their mother, and one of the neighbours told Mari's mother that Mrs Steadman had been crowned Miss Swansea East in 1961 and 1963.

On hot Saturday afternoons while Mari's mother was still on the bus coming home from town with the week's shop, Mrs Steadman would be out in the garden in a pair of tennis-shorts and a bikini top mowing the lawn. As the sun began to sink Mr Steadman would appear from the back of the house with tray of iced drinks and the two of them would sit on the wooden bench in front of their french windows, sipping politely and smoking menthol cigarettes.

He was her second husband. The two girls were away every weekend with their other father who no one ever saw, but everyone imagined must have been very handsome, though poor. Mari believed that Mrs Steadman must still be in love with husband number one, because no one, especially not the beautiful Mrs Steadman, could possibly love Mr Steadman who was a bank manager and was very bald and had a deformed right arm.

It was thought very odd that they should sit in the front of their house even though this was the place that got the sun in the afternoon and evening. Everyone knew that front gardens were just for show and not for sitting in where everyone could see you, but the Steadmans didn't seem to notice this. Nor did they mind that when they put the lights on in the evening everyone could see them sitting down to supper.

On week nights, if Mari had been sent to her room early, she would watch the Steadman family from her window. Sometimes they would all be in different rooms, all with the curtains wide open and the lights blazing. There was Mr Steadman on the sofa in the sitting room reading a newspaper, while in the room next door, Barbara would be practising her piano. Upstairs in the master bedroom, Mrs Steadman could be seen sitting at her dressing table brushing her long silky hair, while next door Bernadette seemed, from her bobbing head and lolloping gait, to be practising some dance steps. Mari could watch them go from room to room, and at moments like that, thought she knew more about them than they did about each other.

The Steadman girls never played on the street. They went to private school and came home late bearing objects like a music case, or tennis rackets, or frothy tu-tus in big plastic bags. Their lives seemed very full and mysterious to

Mari, and she was never quite sure just who had got life right, all the other children with their gangs and games and the stifling ennui of long summer evenings when they were bored witless, or the Steadman girls with their elocution lessons, and tap dancing, and extra tuition. She used to feel sorry for them with all that endless schooling, until one day the Steadman girls had their picture in the paper and Mari's mother had sighed and expressed the wish that Mari could have violin lessons. Mari had felt, when she heard this, that this lack of music classes was due to some failing on her part. When her father had chipped in gruffly, that it would be a waste of time and money, this seemed to confirm for Mari that she, and all the other neighbourhood children, were beyond redemption. That they were scally-wags, poor dabs, dirty mochyns who would never get their photographs in the paper, unless it was for something bad. Like when June's brother Gareth had stolen a double decker bus while the driver was in the cafe, and plowed up the bowling green in a vain attempt to make a get-away.

Mari thought that the Steadman girls would do wonderful things in the future. They'd be models or film stars, and would only come back to Wales to gloat and preen and show off their sports cars and fur coats. When Mari thought about this, she felt regret about not being their friend. She thought that she ought to resent them, hate them even, but instead all she felt was a vivid, admiring, longing. When the other kids shouted names at the girls and pranced about and said in a shriek 'Oh, la-di-da. Lady muck!' Mari was impressed by the way the two girls held their heads up high and tossed their golden manes. It was as if the insults and the name-calling were having the opposite effect of the one intended. The insults only seemed to confirm their elite status on the street, and in the world beyond.

All that changed one day in July of 1969. Mari had just

heard the surprising news that she, contrary to all expectation and hope, had passed her Eleven Plus. She would be going to the girl's Grammar school and her father had promised her ten pounds as a reward. She was upstairs in her bedroom, making a list of things she wanted, when the doorbell rang. She ignored it and wrote 'The Monkees L.P.' then began a drawing of it. She was busy drawing concentric circles on the record when the bell rang again more insistently. She heard the toilet flush, and then her mother shouting 'For goodness sake, someone get the door.' Mari wandered out onto the landing and was halfway down the stairs when her mother rushed past her with the hem of her dress tucked into her knickers. 'Mum,' she said, 'Mum.' But it was too late, her mother had flung open the door and was standing there with her flesh coloured pantie girdle and suspenders and stockings and white puckery skin on show for all the world to see. Except that at that moment, she was thankfully facing the door, and only Mari could see.

Mari went on down the stairs. She couldn't see who was at the door, but as she got closer, she heard an unfamiliar woman's voice. The voice was saying, or slurring rather, 'Oh, god, oh god, oh god, oh Jesus Christ.' It sounded as if the voice was coming from underwater. It lurched and bubbled and choked and spluttered. So far, Mari's mother had said nothing and Mari, sensing that something very unusual was about to happen, and still concerned about her mother's embarrassing exposure, went and stood alongside her at the door.

At first she didn't recognise Mrs Steadman. Her face, besides being very pink and swollen and smeared with black trails of mascara, was contorted in a loose elastic way One half of her hair was in big pink rollers while the other side looked matted and back combed like a big blonde bird's nest. She didn't seem to notice Mari and took a deep gulp of air, then restarted her watery soliloquy, this time with a few more choice words beginning with 'f' and 's' thrown in for good measure.

When she spoke, Mari noticed, in the way one notices the smell of mown grass or perming lotion, that the air was filled with a smell like the smell of a dirty old man who'd once frightened her and June in the park. He'd smelled like that and sworn at them and when he started to unbutton his flies, she and June had ran all the way home. It seemed right that all these things, the smell, and the swearing, and her mother's dishevelled dress, should all happen at the same time.

Mari's mother finally spoke. Mari thought that she would surely tell Mrs. Steadman off for using such bad Language, especially in front of children, but she didn't. She spoke to her softly and said 'Oh dear, oh dear. Whatever is the matter?' Mari felt a pang of betrayal, because it was the voice her mother used with her when she had got stung by nettles or grazed her knees.

Mari's mother told Mrs Steadman to come in, come in, she'd make a cup of tea. Mrs Steadman lurched gratefully forward with something like a smile of thanks on her distorted face, caught her foot on the welcome mat and plunged forward heavily. Mari instinctively jumped back, while her mother clawed uselessly at the air as Mrs Steadman hit the hall floor and lay there moaning.

Mari's mother swung quickly into action. She had driven ambulances during the war, and now for the first time Mari could see some of the old fighting spirit come flooding back. She barked orders at Mari. 'You take that arm. That's, right. Now lift. Okay to your left. Hold her there, have you got her? Hang on.'

They propped Mrs Steadman against the cupboard under the stairs. Mari had to lean against her to keep her upright while her mother went to clear the passage into the best room. Mari watched her mother, as she moved chairs and pushed vases and other valuables out of harm's way. Mari noticed that, somehow, in all the grappling with the very unsteady Mrs Steadman, her mother's dress had unhitched itself from her under-wear and she was restored to dignity, without the embarrassment of anyone telling her.

Mari's shoulder was pushed into the space between Mrs Steadman's breasts while Mrs Steadman's head lolled about and her eyes rolled up in their sockets. She was still moaning and Mari could feel her hot breath blasting the side of her face and smell the horrible smell. She didn't mind so much now, because at least this meant that Mrs Steadman was alive.

Mari's mother was talking as if Mrs Steadman wasn't there.

'Drunk at this time in the afternoon,' she said, 'hold her arm, that's it. Now watch the sideboard, to the settee, and let go. There!' Together, they threw Mrs Steadman onto the leatherette sofa where she bounced in a loose rippling way.

'I'm going to make some strong black coffee. You watch her.'

Mari stood solemnly regarding the heap on the sofa that was the elegant Mrs Steadman. Her cheek was resting on one of the spiky pink rollers, but she didn't seem to mind. Mari wondered if she should adjust it somehow, take it out or put a pillow under her neck, but she had an idea that Mrs Steadman might bite.

Mrs Steadman was muttering something and waving her hand airily in Mari's direction. Mari's mother called out from the kitchen, 'She's not going to be sick is she?'

Mari crept closer and knelt down beside the settee, 'Pardon?' she said. Mrs Steadman finally seemed to notice Mari. Her eyelids fluttered and her mouth twitched in a grimace that seemed a parody of a beauty queen's smile. 'You,' she said, as she groped in vain to pat Mari's head, 'you, my darling, can call me Irene, but don't tell them that.'

Mari's mother came in with the coffee and the two of them tried to sit Mrs Steadman up, but she seemed fast asleep, even when Mari's mother shouted and slapped her face.

'We'll have to leave her, let her sleep it off,' said Mari's mother sipping the black coffee as if she needed sobering up too. 'God knows what's happened. Though really, there's no excuse. I don't know what your father's going to say.' They put a plastic bucket next to the slumbering Mrs Steadman and tiptoed out, even though minutes before, they'd been shaking her and slapping her and screaming her name. Her mother had been saying 'Penelope! Pen – el – oh – pee!' but to no avail. It was only when Mari said "Irene" that there was a flicker of any life. Her mother had looked at Mari oddly when she'd said the secret name, and so Mari had quickly said 'Julie! Diane! Kathy! Rapunzel! Rumpelstiltskin!' and her mother had just shaken her head sadly and said, 'I don't think that will work. She's completely blotto.'

It was very strange that afternoon to be going about their business in the house while Mrs Steadman lay drunk and snoring in the best room with the door wide open in case she threw up and choked. Her mother switched the radio off so that they could listen out for any suspicious noises and Mari stayed close by her mother's side in a way that she hadn't done for years. Her mother was busy making an apple tart, and Shepherd's pie, and a jam sponge. Mari didn't complain, as she usually did, and whine about the fact they never had cream cakes from the bakery. Mari shelled the peas, and they took it in turns to go and look at Mrs Steadman.

They were sitting at the kitchen table playing Rummy and waiting for the cake to cool, when Mrs Steadman appeared. She looked surprised to see them. Her clothes were all rumpled, and she'd taken the curlers out of her hair. Her face looked very pale, except for where the plastic spokes of the curlers had been pressed into her cheek. She was swaying gently and holding onto the edge of the door to steady herself.

'Oh, God,' she said, and Mari thought the awful string of bad language was going to pour forth again.

Mari's mother got to her feet and went and took Mrs Steadman's hand and patted it gently. 'You'll want a shower,' she said. Then as she led Mrs Steadman upstairs, she called back to Mari and told her to make more coffee.

Curiously, this was first time that her mother had allowed Mari to use the kettle on her own without hovering about with morbid tales of scaldings and lifelong disfiguration. Mari felt a surge of pride as she poured the boiling water into the mug without so much as a splash escaping. Upstairs she could hear the shower running and when it stopped she heard Mrs Steadman crying and her mother's voice murmuring, 'There now, you'll soon be right as rain. You can put this behind you and look to the future.'

Mari tried to imagine what Mrs Steadman was putting behind her, at first she had mistakenly thought it must be a towel. She could see it in her mind's eye, her mother passing the big yellow bath towel to a wet naked Mrs Steadman and her explaining to her what to do with it.

When they came downstairs, Mrs Steadman was wearing the quilted nylon dressing gown that always hung on the back of the door in the bathroom, but no one ever wore.

Mari's mother handed the coffee to Mrs Steadman.

'Now you drink that and tell me what the trouble is, my dear. Perhaps I can help in some way?'

Mrs Steadman, looked uncertainly at her, then looked at Mari.

'Sometimes it helps to get things off your chest.'

Mrs Steadman sipped her coffee, then bit her lip. Mari thought she was going to confess to being in love with her first husband still. Her hands trembled as she put the mug on the table.

'It's Geoff,' she said, staring down at her hands as she washed them over each other, 'he's been arrested.'

She let that sink in, before she continued. 'He's been arrested for taking money from the bank.'

Mari pictured Mr Steadman as one of the baddies in a cowboy film, he was wearing a Stetson and pulled a revolver from a holster that was slung around his waist. 'Stick 'em up!' he said, in a voice that was not his own.

It was at that point in the conversation that Mari's mother suggested she go upstairs to do her homework. 'I haven't got any!' Mari protested, but she recognized the tone in her mother's voice as one that would stand firm against any onslaught of opposition.

She trudged back up the stairs, then lay on her bed thinking about the events of the afternoon. She felt weary all of a sudden, and older. She hoped that her mother would tell her the whole story later and if she didn't, maybe she could go over the road and talk to Mrs Steadman herself. She'd say 'Hello, Mrs Steadman. Are you feeling better?' and Mrs Steadman would say again 'Oh, you can call me Irene.'

They'd talk woman to woman, and when the two girls came home, Irene would make them go to their rooms, while she poured Mari a cup of coffee and offered her shop-bought chocolate cream eclairs.

Mari played out this conversation in her imagination again and again. She especially loved the part when Mrs Steadman said 'Call me Irene', and the bereft look on the daughter's faces when they were sent away from the intimate conversation she and their mother would be having. They'd linger at the door staring hatefully at Mari as their mother said again 'You can call me Irene. Do have another eclair, my dear.' And Mari would again say 'Don't mind if I do. Are these from Murray's, Irene?' And she'd reach for the proffered cake, the pastry as light as air, the chocolate cool and glossy and beaded with droplets of moisture, the cream inside heavy and thick and sweet. When Mari bit in, she knew she was tasting some forbidden fruit, but at that moment it didn't matter. She took the cake again and again, and it was always the first bite that was the sweetest.

Ron Jones
Meredith Evans' Kiss

For the record, I am Ernest Jones, poultry farmer, son of
Robert Jones, Deacon, and those are my hens on the hill
above the town. You may eat whomsoever's pigs you wish,
but it is my eggs that you shall be having on your plate if
you sup anywhere in the valley from Park Hamlet right
through Abertridwr. My eggs is on the plates for most the
best part of Caerphilly, too, though I know of some Cardiff
eggs there.

Which is why, of course the boys in the villages, and the
old men, in the villages all down this valley, from
Senghennydd down to Caerphilly, call me Ernie the Egg.
Yes, I am rich, and they make jokes about me. Ernie the
Egg I am, and with a few bob, and sought after by the
Revenue, but I am wealthy by fortunate accidents and hard
work, with the help of God, and because of a great and
ordinary man, Meredith Evans, collier, and because I am
shot in the neck in the Great War and because I am a failed
scholar.

The hens have been my livelihood but this have not
always been so. Once I was to be a teacher, then a collier,
then dead underground, then dead from a bullet in the

Great War. That I am not any of these things is an odd thing for me, peculiar altogether, but facts is facts, which is why I will relate my story.

I was done with school two weeks short of my fourteenth birthday, and was timid, a bit too quiet. I had done an extra year because Robert Griffiths, had persuaded my dada I had a brain and could get a scholarship, but then, when I didn't win a scholarship after all, dada said, 'I am sorry, son, it is time now to earn your keep.' So I was late down.

Because I was late a collier, the other boys marked me as different. They were already pit-hardened, with their broken fingernails and their coal-darkened scars, and they had that look already that the men got from working twelve hours a day in the dark. But me, I still noticed how black they got, and me, I was still afraid of that awful drop in the lift-cage, the way you could feel the earth, and how you knew she smelt you were there, the way the darkness swelled. Too thinking I was, and cursed with it, and the boys knew it and played it up. Which was how it was I became buttied, that is *apprenticed*, to Meredith Twp Evans.

The first thing about Meredith Twp Evans was he was big, and no bones about it, I do mean bloody big. He was huge, slow, shoulders like the back of a milk-cart, fists as big as an apprentice's head, bigger than anyone I ever saw play in the pack for Wales, bigger than anyone I'd seen in all my fourteen years.

But the other thing about Twp was that he was twp, I mean, that is, daft, only half-there, short of a pit-prop or two. They used to say Twp was so twp he didn't even mind being called Twp, and it was true that he had a slow way, in his body, and in his speech and in his head. He was made to push, not to think, and when I started down the Universal, they made me his butty.

I had been set to start as butty to Mr Geraint Williams,

but that first day, frightened enough to faint, I was in the lamp room when one of the boys said something cruel to me and I said something angry back. It was that or cry, and I made a face of it, but Twp saw what was really in that face and said to the foreman, 'Dai, give me Jones.'

Well, Geraint Williams didn't mind either way, so I was switched. Twp grunted, looked at me until I acknowledged him, and then lumbered towards the cage. I ran to put myself alongside him, like I was a pale tug under a huge, dark ship, and even in that place full of the odours of men, I could smell him, the damp grip of underground, strong tobacco, and over it all, the spearmint leaves he chewed.

I was not sure I should live, but I survived that terrible morning, hidden like a lamb in a hollow, in the lee of Twp's huge chest, my eyes closed, my teeth biting my tongue lest I might still cry, my stomach sensing the cage drop and my damn intelligence tormenting me, listening for signs of distress in the winding gear, the physics of the shaft. But I did not die of fear, (as is obvious in me telling this, I know), and months later I was walking to the lamp room at the pit-head to meet Twp. My dreams of being a teacher had faded. I had become a collier.

On the day of the 'Universal' disaster, that was October 14th, 1913, I started at four-thirty. It was damp and dark in the huts, and we ate our bread and blackcurrant jam breakfast while the colliery officials were down for their two hour check (mostly walking and little inspecting, but we knew that). Then it was stamp to work and in our stalls by six. That was the way with piecework; you worked.

I must explain now, for this is a story told looking back, that some things that happened that morning were not as clear in the happening as they are now related. I know, for instance, for I have been told since, that the explosion was just before eight o'clock, and that it was smaller in its first occurrence than the 1901 disaster, but an accumulation of coal-dust in the tunnel ceilings sent death in fizzing jumps towards the levels where we worked.

Duw, but it was a terrible, terrible experience! Some men were crushed under roof falls, some shocked to a quick death by the blast or burned bad by the fire racing along the miles of tunnels. And some were pepper-pocked by a storm of dust that flayed men's arms and faces, in a way so cruel they would have been better dead by flying tools or under one of the many falls.

Our district was the Botanic and we were working the level the miners called Beck's Heading. As the blast roared through, the boys loading trucks were all blown down and tumbled in the wind, not one ever to be a father. By rights I was another dead boy, but Twp had just called me under to help loose some coal. For us under, by chance, and some of the colliers also under, there was only the sudden emptiness of air, and a howl was all for us, like a wounded monster that rushed past us and away into the lampless dark.

I may have fainted, I do not know, but my next recollection was the close breath of spearmint and the voice of Twp calming me, telling me to be still.

I said, 'Twp, what has happened, Twp?' And he told me that there had been a terrific explosion and many were surely killed.

'And we must go out, boy, and walk.'

We crawled out from under. Even now there were thuds and bangs distant, and quick roars of air, but then the air became still and we heard boys crying, and men groaning and it was hopeless, confusion, awful. I was frightened almost dumb. But then I felt Twp's huge hand on my shoulder, and his rough, dirty fingers touching my face. He came close, so close I smelt his chew. 'We must walk,' he said. 'And we must not stop walking.'

'Yes, Twp,' I said.

'Give me your hand,' he said.

And I felt Twp turn his back, then my hand was on his shoulder, taken by his and laid on him like an epaulette, his hand still on mine for comfort, he understood me so well. Then he bade me be silent, and we waited.

Be deliberate quiet for ten seconds against your nature. it is a long time. Do much the same and wait for half a minute, that is an eternity. After a while I thought I would burst from my fear. 'Twp?' I said.

'Shush, boy,' he said.

We waited, but the darkness, the faint crying, were too much and I spoke again. 'Twp?'

Twp did not speak, but I know he turned round. For I felt his fists, now open hands, take my head, my face to his, and I felt his lips on my forehead, not a kiss, but as if Twp was breathing some of his hugeness into me. Very quiet he was. He said, 'Boy, be bigger now for we are suffocating, and there are men here who do not know what to do.'

Then he let me go and called out.

'I am Twp Evans, Newbridge,' he said, big and definite, like a lighthouse blows its horn to guide ships home. 'Shout out, one by one, your name, your stall and are you injured. Is David Thomas spared?'

Thomas answered. 'Yes, but not my buttee.'

'Will Morgan?'

Nothing.

'No? Alun Parry?'

'Yes.'

Like this, we found there were five men, Twp, and me. None bad, but all so tired we each felt like it was Sunday afternoon and a nap by the fire was the thing.

'Get up and walk!' Twp said, 'after-damp is making you silly. If you sleep you will never wake up.'

'Monoxide?' I said half thinking, half-whispering, but Twp did not hear me. He was moving along the heading, punching men's legs, shouting into their faces. 'If you have wives, then get you up and walk!'

The seven of us began to walk but the feelings in us were very strange. My head was half-addled, but from my extra time with Mister Griffiths, teacher, and my Saturdays spent in the library down at Caerphilly I knew, that Twp meant we suffered bad there from monoxide, a poison that kissed men to death, for it smelt of nothing, tasted of nothing, and first it seduced, made them soft, like perhaps they had drunk a little too much. The men wanted to sit down, but to sit down was to die, and now Meredith Twp Evans, after twenty year's of miners' jokes that he was slow to light up, was our intelligence.

'Walk,' he said, 'or feel my fists!'

And the men walked, to sweeter air

It might have been all, that as that, but we still had to get out. The men were now behind Twp, but we were still very tired and the after-damp still whispered to each of us, 'Rest, just a minute, you will feel so much better.'

But Twp insisted. 'Walk!'

Later, I cannot know enough to be exact, but would guess the time to have been perhaps ten o'clock, about then, we came upon an opening, a crossing place for tram-lines, some men and a boy. They were sitting. Their leader was a man called John Pugh, a hard, rough chap known for fighting in the village, and a foreman.

'John Pugh,' Twp said respectfully.

'*Mister* Evans.'

'We have walked, I calculate, best of a mile, Mister Pugh,' Twp said, 'from Beck's Heading along to here, where we have found you. We are looking for better air. The after-damp has gentled too many into a long sleep already.'

'The air is good here, Twp Evans, and safe enough. And here is where rescue is most likely. We should sit.'

'Mr Pugh,' Twp said slowly, 'most respectfully, I do not think the air here is that good.'

'I am foreman,' Pugh said. 'And you are Meredith Twp Evans. I say sit.'

'The air is bad, Mister Pugh.'

'And thou art twp, Mister Twp.'

In the soft darkness, I felt Meredith pause and if there is a sound or a smell to great decisions, I sensed both.

'I will come closer, then John Pugh,' I heard said, very friendly, and in answer, 'Come across, then,' from Pugh, before a scuffle of coal dust, some shout or other, a heavy blow, more blows, and then Meredith speaking.

'Now, I am Twp Evans and the foreman is of an accident and resting. It is time to walk and any man disagrees, he can back his judgement against my fists. You get up now and follow my buttee.'

Dai Pugh was not Twp Evans but he was still a big man. He would be carried or die but none were fit enough to do it. Then Twp spoke. 'Walk on, Ernest Jones!' and I heard him cough, then grunt as he shouldered up the foreman. 'Yes, sir, Mister Meredith!' I said.

At one minute to eight that morning, there had been four hundred and fifty-six men and boys underground and four hundred and thirty eight were killed, one more dead above ground when the cage spat from the shaft and took his head as he was looking down at the sound.

Three hundred had survived the blast, but tall, short, clever or twp, one by one they went to sleep. But Twp Evans saved us and they gave him a medal. On the back it said 'Meredith Evans, Collier, for gallantry' but I say it should have been for intelligence.

When John Pugh woke, we were sixteen of the eighteen spared and were in a pocket, sitting now, but breathing sweeter air, and more likely to be found. At first John Pugh was angry, but Twp whispered to the foreman and they came to an understanding, an arrangement about forgetting. But even this sweeter air was treacherous and when rescue came at last, all of us, even Twp, had given in to the sweet whisper of the monoxide and needed oxygen to return to life.

They brought us out two at a time, into rain, but I asked to stay with Twp and come out last, proud now to be his butty, and me I thought, just a little bigger than I had been at breakfast. But it was into silence, not cheers, for the numbers of certain dead was growing and hope for the rest not so high.

Truth is, after something like that, which only those who experience it can ever hope to understand, to be carried on a litter through the wives, the sweet rain falling, was to wonder at your own fingers and toes, to taste every drop of rain, and to feel and savour every breeze, the flapping of shawls, the crunch of boots in the wet gravel. And I was both terrible sad and terrible proud, almost in the pink, as if I was specially saved and saved because I was special.

Fifteen of us went to The Miners' Rest at Porthcawl, but not Meredith. I was not sure where he was going but he bade me take care of myself and to roll up my trousers if I paddled in the channel. He asked me would I ever go under the ground again and I said to hell first. At that he grinned, pushed his huge fist at me and walked away, his hands in his pockets and him whistling.

But then old Joe Kaiser started up and we were called to service. I was working in a bicycle shop in Fleur-de-Lys, but I went to sign up for the shilling as soon as I could. I was rejected. My lungs, they said, were bad. The after-damp, the accident, all that had made me unfit to serve the King. They had lots of volunteers, they said, but if I worked at my rehabilitation I could try again in three months. I was given a badge to show I was no coward and could drink in peace and was sent away.

It was the same later that year, the same again in 1915, in 1916 and 1917. But then, in the attrition, requirements fell, and in 1918, they took me on, fitted me out in khaki and sent me to France. And I was shot. So laugh at me boys, but I have been underground, and to France, and I was shot.

When a bullet goes by, it's like a buzz, something angry. I heard that buzz. I was with another lilywhite, a Borderer like me, and the bee-zing happened and Arthur went limp. I was too new to think and as I turned to him and bent down to help, I was shot too, no sound, this time, just my face hot, my neck strange and then, within a second I had voided and my legs gave up.

The bullet had missed my head and entered me at the collar, coming out somewhere lower, my backside, and now I could not use my legs. There was never any pain, and never any glory. I had been at the front two days and got a Blighty one. They sent me to Southampton on a stretcher, then on crutches, I came back to Porthcawl, then in 1919, with a walking stick, I went to Barry and they taught me how to keep chickens. That's how I became Ernie the Egg and wealthy, but I have been under the ground and I have been shot for my country. I limp of course, money can't cure that, but I have a daughter and now a grandson, Meredith. I like to walk and I like the sweetness of the air on top of the mountain. I do not like the dark but most times it cannot rain hard enough to disturb me. When it does, I wait in the lee of a mountain and rest, thinking myself twp for being out without a coat. And I wonder about Meredith Evans, collier, but he is gone.

Heather Jones
Tom's Homecoming

Tom pulled on the handles of the patio doors, gently at first. Finding they would not yield to his persistent attentions, he tugged even harder until his hands began to hurt, but still the doors would not budge. Heaving a weary sigh at the futility of his efforts he pressed his nose against the glass and stared at the scene outside. A black cat sat on the neat patio meticulously cleaning it's white blazed breast, oblivious of an onlooker. It paused momentarily to fix a twittering sparrow with a malignant stare. Tom rattled the door once more, hopelessly now. The distracted cat looked up sharply at the noise, then continued it's grooming, forgetting both Tom and the sparrow. It yawned, stretched, then sauntered across the orderly garden. Trotting down the sloping rosebed it crossed the visitors' car park eager for the day's adventures. Tom watched it disappear from view – then began to bang his head softly against the breath misted glass.

The sight of the cat had triggered Tom's memory. He was five years old again, safe in the dim musty parlour of his childhood home, the cat his only companion, the clock ticking loudly and gonging each hour authoritatively. He was feeling glum as he played with a jigsaw puzzle upon the floor. Mother's muffled voice came into his consciousness from the next room where she spoke with friends. Dinner was finished, brothers Alfie and Joe and sister Annie played in the garden with the visiting children. Tom couldn't go out. His chest hurt. Mother said he must play patiently until the others came back indoors. The black cat with the white blazed breast sat on the hearth quietly licking it's fur until Tom rattled the jigsaw pieces searching for a shape. The bright eyed creature purred, rolled onto it's side and watched keenly. Interested green eyes darted from box to puzzle, to box again, following every movement of the little pale fingers. Suddenly, it sat up, alert, ready – then leapt at the irresistible movement, creating a bright red streak upon the pale flesh. Yelping with shock Tom rubbed his hand, ran across to the window to call the children playing outside. He wanted them to come indoors a moment, see his wound, console him. The stiff window catch wouldn't budge so he tapped on the glass. The laughing squealing children couldn't hear. He rapped harder with his fist. Still no-one heard or saw the pouting face at the window. Angry tears began to run down his cheeks as he banged harder. He began to thump his head against the pane of glass over and over again until his mother, hearing the commotion came to his side

'For goodness sake, Tom please come away from that glass. Stop banging your poor old head. The patio doors are locked.' Someone steered him gently away from the doors in another direction. Tom had scratched his hand, there was a thin red line upon the pale thin flesh. He shuffled back down the length of the dayroom passing inelegantly postured bodies propped and slumped in soft plastic armchairs about the room. Drifting into his consciousness, invading his private thoughts, came the snoring, weeping, laughing, rambling and chattering sounds around him, mingling and becoming children playing in a garden somewhere, long ago.

'God luv us!' exclaimed Mavis Hodges as she plumped someone's cushions. 'He'll hurt himself on that door one of these days.' She was addressing the enthusiastic young woman who was following her around that day to learn the duties of a Carer in the Geriatric Unit attached to the hospital of a country market town. The fresh faced young woman, full of compassion, startled by Tom's behaviour, tentatively suggested:

'Perhaps he just wants to go in the garden for a while Mrs. Hodges. I know it's cold, but surely he wouldn't hurt with his coat on? I could walk him round.'

'Look dear, last time we let Tom sit in the garden he went walkabout into town. A policeman brought him back. We've too much to do to sit out there watching him.' As if to verify her statement a fat woman called for assistance, she was wedged in her chair. The young woman spent her first day mopping and wiping, fetching and carrying. She fed the crippled, talked to the lonely and offered comforting words to newcomers crying in corners.

That day Thomas Nathaniel William Brown walked the length of the dayroom seventy-eight times. Once for each year of his life.

Tom perambulated the room every day, his pale blue watery eyes staring fixedly ahead, a wisp of grey hair falling across his wrinkled brow, his brain absorbing the daily sounds of his physical world. The voices of patients, nurses and helpers passed and merged into a hazy cacophony, sometimes triggering memories.

'There you are dear, are you comfortable?'

A lonely voice chastised it's owner, day in, day out, for some past misdemeanor

'I'm a wicked woman, a very wicked woman. I'm a wicked woman....' On and on it went.

'Nurse, Nurse, hurry please, I've got to go, I've got to go.'

On this day another cog moved in Tom's memory.

'But I've got to go.' Brother Alfie was speaking to little sister Annie, sobbing over her breakfast. She held his hand tightly beneath the table where he and brother Joe sat stiffly in their new army uniforms. The three brothers eyes met and Tom bent awkwardly to stroke the cat and hide his adolescent tears from his family. Their mother fussed around them all nervously whilst Father's knife and fork disinterestedly minced the bacon on his plate. He addressed the two proud recruits.

'Well lads, this is a right sad parting, but I'm proud of you both. We all are. I'd be there myself if I were your age.'

'I'll be going too, when I'm older,' Tom said casting a sidelong glance at his father. Joe patted Tom's shoulder.

'You'll be doing a grand job here Tom you've mother and Annie to care for as well as the farm.'

'But I've got to go, I've got to go. If Father won't let me I'll run away,' Tom replied angrily. Breakfast over, the two brothers hugged and kissed their mother and Annie repeatedly, shook Tom's hand vigorously and clasped Father in a long sad farewell. Heaving kitbags across their broad shoulders they marched down the lane without looking back. Tom saw his father weep that day. The weather-reddened cheeks streamed with tears that settled like dew into the coarse greying mustache.

'Come on Tom me lad. We've work to do. Go harness Gypsy, we'll plough top field today.'

In the stable Gypsy stamped, impatient to be away but Tom's heart was not in the work. All day they ploughed up and down top field. The straight deep furrows unfurled behind. Tom thought of his brothers in the trenches – sitting right inside the generous nurturing earth, the life giver. He thought of his brothers in battle, those two ploughers of fields ploughing men into soil. He wondered if all the bodies left in the trenches would be covered over afterwards where they lay and the ground eventually seed as he would seed these furrows. Seeds generated new life he thought, new life from the dead.

'What on earth is Tom doing?' the new worker asked Mrs. Hodges.

'I don't know dear. We've all had a guess, Tom came here from an old farmhouse just a mile outside town, poor old chap lived there alone, terrible run down it was. I believe it had been the family farm and he'd lived there all his life. He never married. My opinion is he's going about here repeating work he used to do on the farm.' She headed towards Tom who paced up and down a harrowed field casting seed by hand, cogitating his plan. He'd run away if his father wouldn't let him enlist. He'd run away to war with Alfie and Joe.

'Tom you'll tire yourself out walking about like this, do come and sit down.' Tom's eyes stared vacantly beyond Mrs Hodges, though he heard her voice. He'd do as his mother said for now, for the time being.

A death occurred overnight but another frail being already waited in the wings to fill the vacant bed, to command and demand the staffs' attention. The morning saw the young woman struggling to placate a new arrival who kept up a constant shrill wail whenever she was left alone. The sound frightened Tom, he sat on the floor hiding behind a chair. He was in the trenches now. He was cold and hungry and wishing he'd never joined up. He yearned for home, for the ploughing and harvesting, for his mother. He didn't want to be in this cold dark hole. Alfie and Joe were dead, killed in action that's what the telegram had said. Now here he was risking his own life. On either side his comrades sniffed, snored, coughed and spat, few spoke, their bodies and minds tense with fear, they simply waited. Suddenly, men were up and running. Tom was running with them, racing along damp furrowed soil, breathing heavily, sweating, afraid. Smoke obscured his vision, deafened by gunfire he was barely conscious of a comrade falling beside him. Then out of the smoke and stench around him came a scream

'Help me, help me. Don't leave me alone,' the voice wailed. Tom stopped abruptly, turned. A Commanding Officer appeared through the smoke, ordered him onward.

'Forward Brown.'

'But Sir, he's alive, he's screaming for help Sir.' Tom couldn't locate the wailing voice. There was too much confusion.

'Go on you bloody fool. That's an order,' the Officer screamed at him.

Tom's face was flattened against the steamed glass of a window staring outside, searching. Mrs Hodges paused briefly in passing to squeeze his soft dry hand comfortingly.

'Tom whatever's the matter? Why are you crying, what are you looking for? Come from the window, you can't go out dear.'

'He's calling for help Sir,' Tom said

'Who is Tom?'

'Calling, I must go to him.'

'You must go back to your table for breakfast Tom, that's an order,' Mrs. Hodges replied.

After the battle Tom's spirits were low. He sat eating his rations with his comrades, resting and thinking. Loneliness had crept into his life, unannounced and uninvited, Father was right to try to keep him from this for as long as possible. He was too young. Would his father ever forgive him for running away to this dreadful war? It couldn't be right to leave a man to die could it? It had been an order though – Father would tell him if he'd done right. They must be finding it hard to manage at home without him what with little Annie to care for too. What good was he here? He hated the army, hated this bloody war, hated the noise. He especially hated the C.O. He wondered if they'd find him if he deserted. He could go back home, hide there safely. This place smelled like a bloody hospital.

Late that afternoon in the Administrator's office Mavis Hodges, feeling both anxious and angry, stood beside the young woman who fidgeted nervously at finding herself in an embarrassing predicament – and this only her second day.

'Of course, I do realise you are short staffed Mrs. Hodges but just how did the patio doors come to be open? You are responsible for keeping them locked.'

'I'm sorry but this young woman decided to take Tom for a stroll round the garden in her teabreak this afternoon, she's been concerned that he's always trying to get out. She took the keys, unlocked the door and was just about to get Tom, when someone attacked Mrs Kilburn because of her constant wailing. She ran to sort things out and in the noise and confusion forgot the doors were unlocked – Tom must have seen. When she remembered Tom she couldn't see him around. By the time she'd checked the toilets and questioned everyone she guessed he'd slipped out closing the doors behind him.' The Administrator's most withering stare was directed at the tearful, crimson faced young woman, who bit her nails enthusiastically.

'Well, we've informed the police of course, they're out looking now. He can't have gone far. I hope for all our sakes, not least his, they find him. It's been a cold day and will soon be dark. I've spoken to the doctor and quite frankly he doesn't think Tom could survive a night out of doors. Has he taken anything with him?'

'Curiously enough, he's taken his dressing gown, it'll be easy enough to spot him in that.'

Tom hurried through the flowerbeds and took a quiet

street that led to the canal. The canal towpath passed at the back of a row of Victorian houses and led in a short while to open countryside. It was good to be out of the dark trenches, out in the cold Spring sunshine. He trudged on doggedly, hands thrust deeply into the pockets of his army greatcoat. He clambered over a stile that brought him onto a path leading towards a wood and disappeared from view. Tom ached with the cold and the effort of crossing a gurgling stream. He came across the familiar sight of a ploughed field, gulls circling above like vultures waiting for him to drop. Stumbling over the damp brown ridges he smiled, his heart filled with the greatest happiness as he made for a hill topped with a copse of birches.

'Got to stop Tom, stop to rest,' he mumbled as he scrambled up the bank. He gasped and wheezed with the effort, his lungs bursting. Reaching the copse he fell to the ground and leant his back against a tree.

'Out of sight here, must rest Tom lad.'

From where he sat he could see the farmhouse. He was home at last. On top field he could see Father with Gypsy. Mother's washing flapped crazily on the line and smoke curled invitingly from the cracked old chimney. He lay down in the cold springtime wood and covered himself with his greatcoat.

'Nearly home Tom, nearly home,' he whispered to himself, closing his pale blue eyes.

Huw Lawrence
Pure Welsh

It's Friday night in the Court Royale, as the place was called at that time. I'm sitting right in the front. The comedian behaves as though he's delighted to see me.

If everyone in Africa held hands around the globe, half the black bastards would drown.

Witty, eh?

Someone asked Stevie Wonder what it's like being blind. It could be worse, he said, I could be black.

Nice fella, this comedian. Rough diamond. Likeable for being a bit tubby.

Hey you. He points to a young farmer with very short hair. *You look like a nice lad, go and piss on that black.* He points at me, but there's not much laughter. *Plane load of Africans crashed, two hundred killed. Broke my fuckin' heart it did. Six empty seats, there was.*

Yes, really witty material. So. I'm looking around to see who's in the audience, and there's this crowd of young farmers there. These have a different idea of what immigration is. And it is something the fat comedian knows nothing about.

... watching Swan Lake. It's where the swan is dying, but

it's a black swan, so bollocks to it anyway....

He's not getting much response and this is the moment he moves away from the mike to a small table holding his glass of water.

Ok. This is my chance!

I'm up on the stage in a trice wearing a smile with the mike in my hand. The surprise on his face turns quickly into a grin. He lifts his palms to the ceiling in a gesture of friendly compliance.

'*Hogia!*' I say in Welsh, 'I've got to tell you this one.'

It's a language the fat comedian doesn't understand one word of. On my lips it produces a surprised silence. All eyes are upon me.

'This is one for patriots. Any Tregaron boys here?'

'*Hwre!*' shout several young farmers.

Remember, I'm speaking in Welsh.

'A fat Englishman, like this one behind me, goes into the red lion with a parrot on his shoulder, right? "Where d'you get that?" asks the barman. "Where the hell have you been living?" says the parrot, "there are dozens of the bastards moving in every month."'

Like a swallow to its nest, that one. A second or two to sink in and there's a riot of laughter. The best of it is, it's one of the fat comedian's own jokes!

My arm is gripped. The microphone is wrenched from my hand and it's back with me to my seat.

'Sssssssss,' hiss my new friends. 'Boo,' they shout. Things begin to look black for the fat comedian. Forgive the pun.

'Bravo,' he grins from the stage, gesturing as if we are colleagues.

I'm on my feet.

'*Hogia*, whose side are you on?' I shout in Welsh.

They shout their support. The place is in uproar.

Then, quick, before worse can happen, I'm between two large fellas heading towards the door with my feet not

110

touching the ground. 'Come on, boys,' I say to them sweetly, in English, 'play the white man.'

'Sorry mate,' says one of them, as they put me through the door. He means it, too. He doesn't like what he's had to do. That's his problem. My problem is, I'm outside. Inside, the young farmers strike up a patriotic song about how the town square isn't big enough for their boys – I mean *our* boys.

When Gwenda my girlfriend comes out after me, I'm astonished. She hadn't accompanied me and I hadn't mentioned my intention of going. Walking down Eastgate I have little to say and Gwenda shows she knows when to keep quiet. Every now and again a thing stands out for what it is. Me, I'm a target. And you, respectable Welsh folk? You've forgotten the *Blue Books*, forgotten what it was like. Your short memory's a big pity for me. You who protest against our language dying forget to protest bigger causes. *Ni wyr y gog ond un ungainc*: the cuckoo only knows one tune.

'Who is he?' I hear some of you ask.

Does it matter? Really, does it?

I let go of Gwenda's hand. I'm glad of my background and my nationality and of her, but right now I'm more comfortable apart.

'Don't react personally,' says Gwenda, taking my hand again. 'You acted politically.'

I make no reply to this.

Friday night in Aberystwyth. The streets are full of young people. Under the streetlights and the stars they shout and laugh as they wander from pub to pub. They are all – I mean, we are all – so similar in dress, ambition and desire, in the global village. Perhaps complete similarity is the answer. But there are beggars drinking cans of lager in the doorways of Smiths and the Spa. Where did they come from? Who are they?

'I hope you're not going to make a habit of nights like tonight,' says Gwenda, squeezing my hand.

Everything makes sense to Gwenda. I think she actually has reasonable feelings. We met at some forgettable performance in the Arts Centre some six months ago, a girl with the Welsh of *Ysgol Rhydfelen* and a black gog whose Welsh is stronger than his English. Of course, she comes from the only Welsh city with a black population. How many Welsh people think of Cardiff blacks as Welsh at all? Her grandparents were Italian. It shows a bit in her colouring and in her hair and black eyes. Gwenda Bracchi, my dark Italian beauty. Her grandfather sold ice-cream in Morriston and learned Welsh, like my father. They got absorbed in only one generation. Then Welsh died out in the family. But now a grand-daughter is taking a degree in it, is a member of The Welsh Language Society and is walking into the future with a black Welshman in a free country.

We turn into North Parade, which is quiet, having no pubs.

'I hadn't planned on seeing you tonight,' I remark.

'You don't say,' she mocks.

'How did you know?'

'I guessed.'

'Hell, how?'

'I know you,' she says.

This moves and disturbs me. I stay silent. At the end of North Parade we turn left and walk towards the Crystal Palace Hotel.

'Did you consider what could have happened?' I ask.

She gives me a peculiar look.

'Why look like that?' I say, 'It could have got violent.'

She's wearing jeans and leather and not much make-up, the kind of outfit she wears on demos. When we arrive at the pub she opens her handbag and puts a brick down by the side of the road. We enter the pub without a word.

It's so crowded you can scarcely move. Waiting to get served at the bar my feelings are a difficult matter. I know Gwenda is too mature for bravado. She was ready to stick up for me, physically. But I still can't allow myself to get too near to her. Detachment continually proves its value. As now, for instance. This little girl with long blond hair and enormous spectacles wants to show that she loves me better than all the other dolls in the Crystal Palace. Pain, that's the problem with feelings.

My father says I must accept pain and learn to deflect it, instead of being a target. You've got to learn that you won't change anything, he says. Don't carry a grudge against experience, just learn to deal with it. Let the past teach you how to handle the present. Remember one thing, he tells me, you're always living Now.

The blue-eyed blond with big glasses, who's drunk, is losing her grip. After talking a great deal she's suddenly become hypersensitive to her own words. It's surprising how often 'black' and 'white' crop up in conversation. In Welsh the word white also means blessed – no prizes for guessing the connotations of black. Anyway, the mirror of language strikes blondie dumb. I am watching this. Others are embarrassed, but I am somewhere else. Wordlessly, she takes my hand and places it on her breast. With her other hand she touches my face. Obviously, we're in a new area, of some ambiguity. Gwenda goes to ring for a taxi. The juke-box is playing 'Hotel California', '...this can be Heaven and this can be Hell....'

'Fuckin' tadpole brain,' says Gwenda, in the taxi.

Gwenda soon forgets my bespectacled Goldilocks and falls into animated conversation with the driver, first in English, then in Irish, which she learns as part of her Celtic Studies. I've noticed every Irishman speaks a little of his own language. As I relax in the back of the taxi Goldilocks swirls among young farmers, drunken students and the under-class in shop doorways. Into my mind come equations. They extend into infinity as language can't, rescuing me for a moment from having to feel. An image of my father appears on the other side of a railway carriage window, running briefly alongside my train, full of pride, seeing his son off, twenty years a clerk in the dole office without promotion... but not me, I say to myself, I'm going to be *somebody*! But I'm in a café, the meaningless writing of rain on the window, listening to a joke about Rastus and Lisa, listening to the sudden silence that interrupts the laughter when I am noticed.

I had a phone call from my father last night. We chatted about the family, a factory cutting its workforce, a quarry re-opening after a century. I could tell something was amiss. I could almost see the groove that appears between his cheek and chin when he's upset.

'And the bowls team?'

'Playing Llan on the weekend for the cup.'

'Fingers crossed then. How are things at work?'

'Fine.'

'Anything new?'

He confessed something small had happened at school, upsetting Meinir, my little sister. 'Thoughtless words on the playground. You know how children can be.'

'Children can be cruel.'

'It was only a small thing.'

'She'll soon forget.'

Even as I spoke the lie I remembered the old saying: '*Peth garw yw cof plentyn*: A child's memory is a painful thing.'

'Children aren't unhappy for long, are they?' asked my father.

'No, dad.'

Foolish Gwenda has brought up the question of

Northern Ireland and our young taxi driver has become silent. His political feelings are his business. He's as distant suddenly as the passenger in the back seat.

Words are what did it.

'It was a small thing,' my father repeated.

Even just one word can do it.

The Contributors

Catherine Merriman is the author of two collections of short stories. Her novel *Leaving the Light On* (Gollancz/Pan) won the Ruth Hadden Award for best first work of 1992, and her story collection *Silly Mothers* was shortlisted for Welsh Book of the Year. She has had many stories broadcast on Radio 4. She lives in Monmouthshire.

Glenda Beagan has lived in Rhuddlan, North Wales, all her life, apart from time spent as a mature student at Aberystwyth and Lancaster. She has published two volumes of short stories, *The Medlar Tree* and *Changes and Dreams* both with Seren, and a collection of poems *Vixen* with Honno. Her work has been translated, broadcast on radio and widely anthologised. In 1999 she won the Trewithen Poetry Prize.

Roger Granelli was born and bred in Pontypridd. Educated at Warwick and Cardiff universities, he has been a professional musician for most of his working life. He has published four novels, most recently *Status Zero*, has received an Arts Council bursary and has had work broadcast on Radio 4. He is currently working on a fifth novel.

Babs Horton was born in Wales and now lives in Plymouth, with her husband, daughter and son. She has worked as a teacher, currently for Plymouth Hospital School. She has won several prizes for her short stories and finished her first novel, *Jarful Of Angels*.

Caryl Ward lives in Llantwit Major and has contributed poems and stories to many magazines and anthologies. Her collection of poetry, *Muddy Eyes*, was published by Red Sharks. At present she is working on a novel.

Deborah Chivers is a creative writing tutor at Cardiff University. She is writing her first collection of short stories, which includes *Radio Baby*. She now writes short stories using the name Deborah Davies.

Lewis Davies is a writer and publisher. His work includes the plays *My Piece of Happiness* and *Without Leave* and the books *Work, Sex and Rugby* and *Tree of Crows*. He won the John Morgan Award for his travel book *Freeways: A Journey on Route 66* and the Rhys Davies award for 'Mr Roopratna's Chocolate'. Despite several attempts to escape he lives in Cardiff.

Joyce Herbert read English at the University of Wales, Cardiff and after a career in teaching is now living in the Vale of Glamorgan. Her poetry has appeared in *Anglo-Welsh Review, Poetry Review, Poetry Wales, Stand, The Jewish Quarterly, Poetry Ireland Review, New Poetry*, The Arts Council of Great Britain's *New Poetry, The Dybbuk Delight, Poetry Wales: 25 Years, Burning the Bracken, Twentieth Century Anglo-Welsh Poetry*. A collection *Approaching Snow* was published by Poetry Wales Press. Her stories have been commissioned for broadcasting and have appeared in *Stand, Madog* and the Arts Council of Great Britain's *New Stories*. She also won a Welsh Arts Council award for short stories.

Rae Howells, at 22 years of age, might be the last person you'd expect to find writing a short story about an elderly lady with senile dementia. Luckily, nature has furnished her with the two essential qualities every writer should have: imagination and ambition. With this winning combination behind her, she is currently completing her first novel, written as part of Manchester University's Novel Writing MA, and which she hopes will provide her with the cash to pay her mascara bill for a number of weeks at the very least. She lives, works and writes in Mumbles, Swansea.

Jo Hughes was born and raised in Swansea, and has also lived in Aberystwyth and London. Her stories have been broadcast on Radio 4, published in various magazines and anthologies, and have won or been shortlisted for a number of competitions including the Asham and the 1995 Rhys Davies Short Story Competition.

After surviving the Clapham rail disaster in December 1988 and a period of Post Traumatic Stress, **Ron Jones** gave up a career in computing to write full time. His many publications include five novels, and literary short stories in *The New Welsh Review, Western Mail, The Mississippi Review* and *Atlantic Monthly*.

Heather Jones lives in rural Mid-Wales. She describes herself as a 'non-serious scribbler since childhood.' After raising a family she abandoned self-sufficiency to work part time, travel, and relax! 'Tom's Homecoming' was her first attempt at writing for a competition and inspired by this success she went on to write poetry. Her first poem was accepted for an anthology and another was recently short-listed in an international competition. Her ambition is to write a humorous book – and to win more prizes.

Huw Lawrence was born in Llanelli in 1942. He took a BA and an MA at Manchester University before settling for a life in the teaching profession, taking early retirement from Coleg Ceredigion in 1993. He has had poems and stories published in various magazines, including *Planet*,

The Anglo-Welsh Review, The New Welsh Review and *Poetry Wales*. He has two sons and lives in Aberystwyth with his wife of thirty years.